The critics on Jostein Gaarder's
previous international bestseller
Sophie's World

'A marvellously rich book. Its success boils down to something quite simple – Gaarder's gift for communicating ideas'
Guardian

'An Alice in Wonderland for the 90s . . . already *Sophie's World* is being talked up as philosophy's answer to Stephen Hawking's *A Brief History of Time* . . . this is a simply wonderful, irresistible book'   *Daily Telegraph*

'Remarkable . . . what Jostein Gaarder has managed to do is condense 3000 years of thought into 400 pages; to simplify some extremely complicated arguments without trivialising them . . . *Sophie's World* is an extraordinary achievement'
Sunday Times

'Challenging, informative and packed with easily grasped, and immitable, ways of thinking about difficult ideas'
Independent on Sunday

'*Sophie's World* is a whimsical and ingenious mystery novel that also happens to be a history of philosophy . . . What is admirable in the novel is the utter unpretentiousness of the philosophical lessons . . . which manages to deliver Western philosophy in accounts that are crystal clear'
Washington Post

'A terrifically entertaining and imaginative story wrapped round its tough, thought-provoking philosophical heart'
Daily Mail

'Seductive and original . . . *Sophie's World* is, as it dares to congratulate itself, "a strange and wond

Jostein Gaarder was born in Oslo in 1952. *Sophie's World*, the first of his books to be published in English, has been published in 40 languages and has been a bestseller in each of them.

By the same author

Sophie's World
The Solitaire Mystery
The Christmas Mystery
Vita Brevis
Hello? Is Anybody There?

Through a Glass, Darkly

JOSTEIN GAARDER

Translated by Elizabeth Rokkan

PHOENIX

A Phoenix Paperback
First published in Great Britain by
Phoenix House in 1998
This paperback edition published in 1999 by Phoenix
a division of Orion Books Ltd,
Orion House, 5 Upper St Martin's Lane,
London WC2H 9EA

A CIP catalogue record for this book
is available from the British Library.

ISBN: 0 75380 673 8

Typeset at The Spartan Press Ltd,
Lymington, Hants
Printed and bound in Great Britain by
Clays Ltd, St Ives plc

Joy is a butterfly
Fluttering low over the earth,
    But sorrow is a bird
With big, strong, black wings.
    They lift you high above life
Flowing below in sunlight and growth.
    The bird of sorrow flies high
To where the angels of grief keep watch
    Over death's lair.

Edith Södergran (1892-1923)
(A poem from her notebook written
when she was sixteen years old)

THEY had left the bedroom door open. Cecilia could smell the Christmas smells wafting up from the floor below. She tried to count them.

One was the sweet-sour smell of spicy cabbage. Another must be the incense Father had put on the hearth before they went to church. And could that be the fresh scent of the Christmas tree?

Cecilia breathed in again. She thought she recognised even the smell of the presents under the tree, of red and shiny gold Christmas wrapping paper, gift labels and ribbons. But there was yet another – a vague scent of something enchanting and magical. Christmas itself!

As she smelt all these things she played with the doors in the Advent calendar above her bed. All twenty-four doors were ajar. She had opened the biggest one today. Yet again she looked at the angel leaning over the crib with the baby Jesus. Mary and Joseph stood in the background, but they seemed to be taking no notice of the angel.

Could it be that the angel was invisible to Mary and Joseph?

She looked round the room. Cecilia had looked so often at the red lampshade hanging from the ceiling, the white curtains with blue forget-me-nots and the bookshelf with her books and dolls, crystals and precious stones, it had all become a part of herself. On the desk in front of the window lay the travel guide from Crete beside the old Children's Bible and Snorre's tales of the Norse gods. On the wall between her and her parents' bedroom hung the Greek calendar with the sweet little cats. On the same hook she had hung the old pearl necklace Grandma had given her.

However many times had she counted the twenty-seven rings on the curtain rod? Why were there thirteen rings on the one side and fourteen on the other? How often had she tried to count the copies of *Science Illustrated* lying in a big pile under the desk? She had had to give up every time. She had stopped trying to count the flowers on the curtains. There were always a few forget-me-nots hidden in the folds.

Under the bed lay her Chinese diary. Cecilia felt for it with her hand . . . Yes, her pen was there too.

The Chinese diary was a small notebook covered with material that she had been given by the doctor at the hospital. When she held it up to the light the black, red and green silk threads glittered.

She hadn't had the strength to write very much in the diary, nor had she very much to write about, but she had decided to make notes of all the ideas that came to her while she lay in bed. She had promised herself never to cross anything out; every single word was to stay there till the Day of Judgement. It would be strange to read her diary when she was grown up. Over the whole of the first page she had written: CECILIA SKOTBU'S PERSONAL NOTES.

She flopped back on to her pillow again, and tried to hear what was going on downstairs. Now and then Mother picked up some cutlery, otherwise the house was completely silent . . .

The others would be arriving home from church any minute. Just before – or just after – the bells would ring Christmas in. You could hardly hear the church bells from Skotbu. They always went out on to the doorstep to hear them better.

This year Cecilia couldn't stand on the doorstep listening to the bells ringing in Christmas. She was ill, and she wasn't just mildly ill, as she had been in October and November. Now Cecilia was so ill that Christmas was like a handful of sand that only trickled through her fingers while she slept or was half-awake. At least she didn't have to be in hospital. There they had put up the Christmas decorations at the beginning of December.

It was a good thing she had known Christmas before. Cecilia thought the only thing in the whole world that didn't change was Christmas at Skotbu. For a few days people did the same things they had done year after year, without having to think about why. 'It's the tradition,' they said. That was reason enough.

During the past few days she had tried to follow what was going on downstairs. The sounds of baking and decorating had come up from below like small bubbles of noise. Sometimes Cecilia had imagined that the ground floor was the earth and that she was in heaven.

Yesterday evening they had brought in the Christmas tree; then Father had decorated it after Little Lars had gone to bed. Cecilia hadn't seen it yet. She hadn't seen the Christmas tree!

It was a good thing she had a little brother who was a chatterbox. He talked about everything that the others merely saw or thought about. So he had chattered on about all the preparations and the Christmas decorations. He had been Cecilia's secret reporter from the underworld.

She had been given a bell for the bedside table. She rang it when she wanted to go to the loo or needed something. Usually it was Lars who answered it first. Sometimes Cecilia had rung the bell just so he could tell her what they had been baking or decorating.

Father had promised to carry Cecilia downstairs to the living room when it was time to open the presents. She wanted new skis. The old ones barely reached up to her chin. Mother had suggested that she should wait until she was well again, but Cecilia had protested. She wanted skis for Christmas, and that was that!

'You may not be able to go skiing *this* winter, Cecilia.'

She had thrown a vase of flowers on to the floor.

'Of course I can't go skiing if I haven't any skis.'

Mother had just brought a dustpan and brush without saying a word. That was almost the worst thing about it. As she swept up the flowers and the fragments of glass she said, 'I thought you'd prefer something exciting that you could have with you while you're in bed.'

There was suddenly a tight feeling in her head. 'Have with me while I'm in bed!' So then she had pushed a plate and a glass of juice on to the floor as well. Mother didn't get cross then, either. She had merely swept and brushed, brushed and swept.

To be on the safe side Cecilia had added that she wanted skates and a toboggan as well . . .

Out of doors the cold weather had lasted since the beginning of December. Occasionally Cecilia had crawled out of bed and crept to the window all by herself. The snow lay like a soft quilt over the frozen landscape. Out in the garden Father had put Christmas lights in the big pine tree specially for her. The lights always used to be in the small fir tree by the front door. Between the branches of the pine she could glimpse Ravens' Hill in the distance.

The outlines of the landscape had never been clearer than during these last days before Christmas. Once Cecilia had seen the postman coming on his bike, even though it was almost ten degrees below freezing and there were snowdrifts on the road. At first she had smiled, tapped on the window pane and waved to him. He had looked up and waved back with both arms, then his bike had overturned in the loose snow. As soon as he disappeared behind the barn she had crept back to bed and cried. It had seemed as if the whole meaning of life was a postman cycling in the snow.

There had been another time when tears came into her eyes as she stood in front of the window. She had wanted so much to run out into the magical winter weather. In front of the barn door two bullfinches had been hopping backwards and forwards in a complicated dance. Cecilia had started to laugh. She would like to have been a bullfinch herself. Then she felt tears welling up in the corners of her eyes. Finally she picked up a tear with her finger and drew an angel on the window pane. When she realised that she had drawn the angel with her own tears she had to laugh again. What was the difference between angel tears and tear angels?

She must have dozed off, for she was suddenly woken by the sound of the front door opening.

They were back from church! Cecilia could hear them stamping the snow off their boots. Couldn't she hear the bells ringing as well?

'Happy Christmas, Mama!'

'Happy Christmas, little one!'

'A Happy Christmas to you too, Toni.' Grandad cleared his throat. 'I can smell Christmas dinner!'

'You take his coat, Lars.'

Cecilia could see them in her mind's eye. Grandma smiling and hugging them all, Mama taking off her red apron as she hugged Grandad, Papa stroking Lars's hair, Grandad lighting a cigar . . .

If Cecilia was good at anything now, it was seeing with her ears.

The excitement on the ground floor was interrupted by quiet whispers. The next moment Father was on his way up the stairs. He took them in four or five strides.

'Happy Christmas, Cecilia!'

He put his arms round her and hugged her gently. Then he crossed the room quickly and opened the window wide.

'Can you hear them?'

She raised her head from the pillow and nodded.

'So it must be five o'clock.'

He closed the window and sat down on the edge of the bed.

'Am I going to get new skis?'

It was as if she hoped he would say no. Then she'd have another chance to be angry, and that felt almost better than being sorry for herself.

Father put a finger to his lips.

'No special favours, Cecilia. You'll have to wait and see.'

'If I must, then I must.'

'Are you sure you don't want to lie on the sofa while we're having dinner?'

She shook her head. They had talked about that lots

of times during the past few days. It was better to be rested by the time they came to the presents. She couldn't face eating any Christmas food; it would only make her sick.

'But leave all the doors open!'

'Of course!'

'And you must talk loudly . . . and make lots of noise at the table.'

'I should think so.'

'And when you've finished reading the Christmas Gospel, Grandma is to come up and read it to me.'

'We agreed on that.'

She sank back on to the big pillow.

'Would you give me the Walkman?'

He went to the bookcase and handed her the cassette and the player.

'I can manage the rest myself.'

Father kissed her on the forehead.

'I'd much prefer to sit here with you,' he whispered. 'But there are the others, you see. I'll have to keep you company the rest of Christmas instead.'

'I said you must celebrate Christmas just as usual.'

'Just as usual, yes.'

He tiptoed out.

Cecilia put a tape of Christmas carols in the Walkman. Soon her ears had soaked up all the lovely Christmas atmosphere from the music. She took off the headset, and now – yes, they were sitting at the table.

Mother was reading the Christmas Gospel. When she had finished they sang 'Oh come, all ye faithful.'

Then Grandma was on her way upstairs. Cecilia had planned it all.

'Here I am, Cecilia!'

'Shh! You must just read to me . . .'

Grandma sat on a wooden chair beside the bed and read:

' "And it came to pass in those days, that there went out a decree from Caesar Augustus, that all the world should be taxed . . . " '

When she looked up from the Bible, Cecilia had tears in her eyes.

'Are you crying?'

She nodded.

'But it's not sad.'

Cecilia nodded again.

' "And this shall be a sign unto you. You shall find a babe wrapped in swaddling clothes, lying in a manger." '

'You think it's *beautiful*?'

Cecilia nodded for the third time.

'We cry when something's sad,' said Grandma after a while. 'And we often shed a tear when something's beautiful too.'

'But we don't laugh when something's ugly?'

Grandma had to think about that.

'We laugh at clowns because they're funny. Sometimes I expect we laugh because they're ugly too . . . Look!'

She screwed up her face into a dreadful grimace, which made Cecilia laugh.

Grandma continued. 'Perhaps we're sad when something's beautiful because we know it won't last for ever. Then we start to laugh when something's ugly because we understand it's only a joke.'

Cecilia stared up at her. Grandma was the cleverest person in the whole world.

'Now you must go down to the other clowns,' she said.

Grandma straightened her pillow and stroked her cheek.

'I'm looking forward to you coming down too. Now we're just going to eat . . . '

When Grandma had gone, Cecilia felt for the pen and the Chinese notebook. At the very beginning she had written:

I am not standing on a strange beach in the Aegean Sea any more. But the waves are still breaking on the beach, making the stones roll forwards and backwards, changing places through all eternity.

She quickly read through everything she had written up to now. Then she wrote:

We cry when something is sad. Then we often shed a tear when something's beautiful as well. When something's funny or ugly, we laugh. Perhaps we are sad when something is beautiful because we know that it won't last for ever. Then we start laughing when something is ugly because we understand that it's only a joke.

Clowns are funny to look at because they're so dreadfully ugly. When they take off their clown masks in front of the mirror, they become very handsome. That's why clowns are so sad and unhappy every time they go into their circus caravans and slam the door behind them.

She dozed off again and didn't wake up until Father came to fetch her.

'Time for the presents!' he announced.

He put his arms under Cecilia and lifted her up high along with her red duvet. He didn't take the pillow, so her fair hair hung down towards the floor. It had grown very long again.

Grandad and Little Lars were standing at the foot of the stairs.

'You look like an angel,' said Grandad. 'The duvet is like a rosy cloud.'

' "The angel of the Lord came down",' sang Lars.

Cecilia turned her head and met their gaze.

'What a load of rubbish!' she protested. 'Angels sit on *top* of the clouds. They don't hang underneath them, surely?'

Grandad chuckled, and answered her by blowing out a thick cloud of cigar smoke.

Father put Cecilia down on the red sofa. They had piled it high with cushions so that she could see the

Christmas tree. She examined it carefully.

'That's not the star we had last year.'

Mother hurried over – as if she was sorry that everything wasn't the same as last year.

'No, d'you know, we couldn't find it. Father had to buy a new one.'

'That's strange . . .'

Cecilia looked all round the room, and the others watched her, following the direction of her eyes and looking at all the things she saw.

There wasn't a dark corner. Cecilia counted twenty-seven lighted candles – exactly as many as the rings on the curtain rod upstairs. Wasn't that an odd coincidence?

Under the tree lay all the parcels. The only difference from last year was that Grandad wasn't going to be the Christmas *nisse*. Cecilia had decided that too.

'I don't think I can be bothered with that Santa Claus nonsense, you know!'

The table was laid with plates and coffee cups, cake dishes and home-made marzipan figures in different colours.

'Would you like anything to eat?'

'Maybe a little lemonade. And a cookie without any strawberry whip.'

They were all standing round her, Little Lars behind the others. He seemed to find it scary that Cecilia had come downstairs to be with them when they opened their presents. At any rate he looked very solemn.

'Happy Christmas, Lars.'

'Happy Christmas.'

'Now for the presents,' said Grandad. 'I'm the one who's been told I may give them out.'

They sat round the tree, and Grandad began reading the labels. Cecilia noticed that none of the parcels looked like a toboggan or a pair of skis, but she would have to wait to sulk on that account. Something might come out of a hiding place somewhere else in the house. That had happened before.

'To Cecilia from Marianne.'

Marianne was her best friend. She lived on the other side of the river Leira, but they were in the same class.

It was a tiny packet. Could it be jewellery? Maybe it was something to add to her collection of stones . . .

She tore off the paper and opened a yellow box. On a little piece of cotton wool there lay a red butterfly, a brooch. Cecilia took it out of the box, but as soon as she touched it, it changed colour from red to green. Soon it turned blue and purple too.

'A magic butterfly!'

' . . . that changes colour when the temperature changes,' nodded Father.

All of them had to hold it. When they held it tight in the palm of the hand it turned green and blue. Only in Cecilia's hand did it become purple.

'It's a fever butterfly,' said Lars, but they all pretended they hadn't heard him.

The next parcel was for him, a pair of mini-skis from Aunt Ingrid and Uncle Einar.

'I'd rather have had proper skis,' said Cecilia. 'But that's OK by me.'

Now things began to go fast. As the number of parcels under the Christmas tree dwindled, so the chairs and tables began to fill with all kinds of things. Father collected the paper and stuffed it into a black plastic bag.

Then Grandad had to go out. The grown-ups drank coffee, Lars drank pop, Cecilia took her medicine.

When Grandad came back to the living room he was carrying something long and heavy, packed in blue Christmas paper with gold stars on it.

Cecilia drew herself up on the sofa.

'Skis!'

'To the ski champion from Grandma and Grandad,' read Grandad.

'Ski champion?'

'Or ski star,' explained Grandma. 'That's you, you know.'

Cecilia tore off the paper. The skis were as red as the Christmas paper had been blue.

'Super! I wish I could try them out this minute.'

'Well, we must hope you'll soon be up and about again.'

From now on Cecilia kept her skis beside her on the sofa while the rest of the parcels were given out. The last one was so big that it had to be brought in from outside, and it was for Cecilia as well. She guessed what it was as soon as she saw it.

'A toboggan! You're crazy . . . '

Mother leaned over and pinched her cheek.

'D'you think we'd have dared give you anything else?'

She shrugged.

'You didn't dare give me skates.'

'Well, we did take that risk.'

And now it was time for the long, after-dinner coffee. Cecilia was thrilled to see the dishes of cakes and fruit, of marzipan, home-made sweets, and nuts. It was exactly as it should be. It was Christmas. But she only ate a piece of raisin bread herself, and asked for a slice of toast with honey.

Grandad told them about Christmas in the old days. He had celebrated Christmas in that room every single year for more than sixty years. But one year *he* had been ill too.

When the time came for carols round the Christmas tree Cecilia had begun to be drowsy, and she wanted to be carried up to her room again.

First Lars and Mother went up and down with all the presents. Cecilia insisted on having them all with her. Finally, Father carried her upstairs after they had wished each other a happy Christmas tomorrow as well.

So Cecilia fell asleep, while the sound of the carols as the others circled the tree bubbled up from below. Grandma was playing the piano.

CECILIA woke up suddenly. It must be the middle of the night, because the house was completely quiet. She switched on the light above her bed.

She heard a voice asking, 'Have you slept well?'

Who was it? Nobody was sitting on the chair beside the bed. Nobody was standing in the room either.

'Have you slept well?' said the voice again.

Cecilia pulled herself up and looked around her. Then she froze. A figure was sitting on the windowsill. There was only room for a small child, but it wasn't Lars. So who could it be?

'Don't be afraid,' said the stranger in a high, clear voice.

He or she was wearing a white tunic and had bare feet. Cecilia could only just glimpse a face against the bright light from the tree outside.

She tried rubbing her eyes, but the white-clad figure was still sitting there.

Was it a girl or was it a boy? Cecilia wasn't quite

sure, because he or she didn't have a single hair on its head. She decided that it must be a boy, although she could just as easily have decided the opposite.

'Can't you tell me whether you've slept well?' repeated the mysterious visitor.

'Yes, of course . . . But who are you?'

'Ariel.'

Cecilia rubbed her eyes again.

'Ariel?'

'Yes, that's who I am, Cecilia.'

She shook her head.

'I still don't know who you are.'

'But we know nearly everything about you. It's just like a looking-glass.'

'Like a looking-glass?'

He leaned forward, looking as if at any moment he might tip over and fall on to the desk.

'You see only yourselves. You can't see what's on the other side.'

Cecilia gave a start of surprise. When she was smaller she had often stood in front of the bathroom mirror and imagined there was another world on the other side of the glass. Sometimes she had been afraid that the people who lived there might be able to see through the glass and spy on her while she was washing. Or even worse: she had wondered whether they could jump through the glass and appear in the bathroom.

'Have you been here before?' she asked.

He nodded solemnly.

'How did you get in, then?'

'We get in everywhere.'

'Father always locks the door. In winter we shut all the windows.'

He dismissed this.

'Things like that don't bother us.'

'Things like that?'

'Locked doors and that sort of thing.'

Cecilia considered for a while. She felt as if she had been watching some kind of trickery in a film. So she ran the film backwards and went through it once again.

'You say "we" and "us",' she pointed out. 'Are there so many of you?'

He nodded.

'Very many, yes. You're getting warmer!'

But Cecilia was tired of riddles. She said, 'In the whole world there are five billion people. And I've read that the world is five billion years old. Have you thought about that?'

'Of course. You come and go.'

'What did you say?'

'Every single second some brand-new children are shaken out of the sleeve of God's jacket. Hocus pocus! Every single second some people disappear too. A long, long line. O U T spells out, and out you must go.'

She felt her cheeks turning hot.

'You come and go yourself,' she said.

He shook the little head with no hair emphatically.

'Did you know that this room was once your grandfather's bedroom?'

'Of course. But how did *you* know that?'

He had begun swinging his legs. Cecilia thought he looked like a doll.

'Now we've got going,' he announced.

'On what?'

'You didn't tell me whether you had slept well. But we've got going all the same. It always takes a little time to get going properly.'

Cecilia took a deep breath – and let it all out again. She said, '*You* didn't tell *me* either how you knew this was Grandad's bedroom.'

' "How you knew this was Grandad's bedroom",' repeated Ariel.

'That's what I said.'

He kicked his legs over and over again.

'We've been here since the dawn of time, Cecilia. When your grandad was small he was in bed all one Christmas with serious pneumonia, and that was long before proper medicines existed.'

'Were you here then, as well?'

He nodded.

'I shall never forget those sad eyes of his. They looked like two lost baby birds.'

' "Like two lost baby birds",' sighed Cecilia.

She looked up at him and added hurriedly, 'But it passed. He got completely well again.'

'Yes, completely well again.'

He made a sudden movement. In a fraction of a second he had stood up on the windowsill, filling almost the whole window frame. Cecilia still couldn't see his face properly because of the strong light in her eyes.

How had he managed to lift himself up without falling on top of the desk? It seemed as if he couldn't fall down.

'I remember all the shepherds in the field too,' he said.

Cecilia thought about what Grandma had read from the Bible.

'"Glory to God in the highest and peace on earth to men of goodwill",' she quoted. 'Is that what you're thinking about?'

'The hosts of heaven, yes. There was a whole crowd of us there, cheering.'

'I don't believe you.'

Ariel put his head on one side, and now Cecilia could glimpse his face a little better. It reminded her of the face of one of Marianne's dolls.

'Poor you,' he said.

'Because I'm ill?'

He shook his head.

'I mean, it must be horrid not to believe the person you're talking to.'

'Don't care!'

'Is it true that sometimes you're so suspicious, you turn quite black inside?'

She made a cross face.

'I was only asking,' he assured her. 'Even though we've seen how humans come and go, we don't know exactly how it feels to be made of flesh and blood, you see.'

Cecilia squirmed in her bed. But Ariel was not going to give up.

'Isn't it just a bit horrid to be so suspicious?'

'It must be even more horrid to tell such barefaced lies to a girl who's ill.'

He put a hand to his mouth and gave a frightened gasp.

'Angels don't tell lies, Cecilia!'

Now it was her turn to gasp for breath.

'*Are* you really an angel?'

He gave a quick nod – as if this was nothing to boast about. Cecilia became more subdued at once. After a few seconds she said, 'That's what I thought all along. It's quite true. But I didn't dare ask in case I was mistaken. You see, I'm not quite sure whether I believe in angels.'

He brushed this aside with his arm.

'I don't think we need play that game. Imagine if I were to say that I wasn't quite sure whether I believed in you. It would be quite impossible to prove which one of us was right.'

As if to demonstrate that he was a healthy angel, able to be up and about, he jumped down on to the desk in front of the window and began to walk to and fro on the table-top. A couple of times it looked as if he was going to lose his balance and fall to the floor, but he always righted himself again at the very last moment. Once it looked as if he righted himself just *after* the very last moment.

'"An angel in the house",' murmured Cecilia to herself – as if it was the name of a book she had read.

'We call ourselves simply God's children,' replied Ariel.

She stole a glance at him.

'You are, at any rate.'

'What do you mean by that?'

Cecilia tried to sit up a little higher in bed, but she fell back heavily on to the pillow again. She said, 'You're only a child angel.'

He laughed almost silently.

'What's so funny about that?' she asked.

'"Child angel." Don't you think that's an obviously funny description?'

Cecilia didn't know why she didn't think it was so very funny.

'After all, you're not a grown-up angel,' she said. 'So you must be a child angel.'

Ariel laughed again, this time a little louder.

'Angels don't grow on trees,' he said. 'In fact, we don't grow at all. So we can't be "grown-up" either.'

'I'm not going to listen to any more!' exclaimed Cecilia.

'That would be a pity, since I think we're getting on very well.'

'But I thought nearly all angels were grown-up,' she insisted.

Ariel shrugged his shoulders.

'That's not your fault. You can only guess what's on the other side.'

'D'you mean grown-up angels don't exist?'

He went into peals of laughter. It reminded her of how it sounded when Lars dropped his marbles all over the kitchen floor. This time at least she wouldn't have to help him pick them all up.

'So there's not a single grown-up angel,' she decided. 'That's OK by me, but there can't be a single proper priest either, because all the priests boast that there are swarms of grown-up angels in heaven.'

For a moment there was silence. Then Ariel stretched out one arm with an elegant movement.

' "There are swarms of grown-up angels in heaven"!' he exclaimed. ' "Swarms"!'

When Cecilia didn't answer at once he said, 'It's super talking to you, Cecilia.'

She had begun biting her thumb. Then she couldn't help saying, 'I wonder how it feels to be grown-up.'

Ariel sat down on the desk with his bare legs hanging over the edge.

'Do you want to talk about that?'

She lay staring up at the ceiling.

'My teacher says childhood is only a stage on the way to being grown-up. That's why we have to do all our homework and prepare ourselves for grown-up life. Isn't that silly?'

Ariel nodded. 'Because it's really the other way round.'

'What is?'

'It's being grown-up that's only a stage on the way to more children being born.'

Cecilia had a good think before she replied.

'But the grown-ups were created first. If they hadn't been, there would have been no children.'

Ariel shook his head.

'Wrong again. The children were created first; if they hadn't been, there would have been no grown-ups.'

Cecilia had a clever idea.

'The question is, what came first: the chicken or the egg?'

He had started swinging his legs again.

'Do you really still bother about that old riddle? I heard it for the first time from an old chickenherd in India, but that was several thousand years ago. He was bending over a chicken that had just laid a large egg. Then he started to scratch his head. "I wonder which came first," he said, "the chicken or the egg."'

Cecilia looked up at Ariel, at a loss, and the angel explained, 'Naturally the egg had to come first.'

'Why?'

'If it hadn't, there wouldn't have been any chicken. You surely don't think the first chicken in the world came flapping out of thin air?'

Cecilia's head was beginning to spin. She didn't know whether she had understood everything the angel had said, but what she *had* understood sounded perfectly correct. At last she had solved that old riddle, she thought. If only she could manage to remember everything until tomorrow . . .

'That's how it is with children too,' continued Ariel. 'They're the ones who come into the world first. The grown-ups always come limping after. Limping more and more the older they get.'

Cecilia thought that what Ariel was saying was so wise she wanted to write it all down in her Chinese notebook, so as not to forget it. But she didn't dare do it while the angel was watching. She said, 'But Adam and Eve were grown-up.'

Ariel shook his head.

'They *became* grown-up. That was the great mistake. When God created Adam and Eve they were inquisitive little children who climbed trees and played around in the big garden he had just made. There was no point in owning a big garden if there were no children to play in it.'

'Is that true?'

'I've told you, angels don't tell lies.'

'Tell me more, then!'

'So they were tempted by the serpent to eat of the Tree of Knowledge, and then they began to grow. The more they ate, the more they grew. That's how they were gradually driven out of their childhood paradise.

The little rogues were so hungry for knowledge that, in the end, they ate themselves out of Paradise.'

Cecilia gaped, and Ariel looked down at her with an indulgent look.

'But of course you've heard all this before,' he said.

She shook her head.

'I've heard that Adam and Eve were driven out of Paradise, but nobody told me that it was from their *childhood* paradise.'

'You might have been able to guess some of it yourself. But humans understand only in part. You see everything through a glass, darkly.'

Cecilia lay smiling mischievously.

'I think I can imagine little Adam and little Eve running about among the trees in that big garden once upon a time.'

'What did I say?'

'What did you say?'

'You're quite clever at guessing after all. Did you know that humans use only a small percentage of their brains?'

Cecilia nodded, for she had read precisely that in *Science Illustrated*. 'I'd like to hear more about Adam and Eve,' she begged.

At last she had managed to push herself a bit higher up in bed. Ariel went on swinging his legs as he talked.

'At first they started to grow and stretch all their limbs. Then they became sexually mature. That was part of the punishment, but it was a consolation for God, and for humans too.'

'Why was that?'

'Because new people could be brought into the world. And that's how it's been throughout all ages ever since. That's how God has seen to it that children are continually being born who can discover the world anew. In that way he has arranged that creation is never-ending. The world is created anew, you see, every time a child comes into the world.'

'Because when a child comes into the world, in a way the world is quite new for that child?'

He nodded. 'You could just as well say that the world comes to the child. To be born is the same as to be given a whole world – with the sun by day, the moon by night, and the stars in the blue sky. With an ocean that washes in over the beaches, with forests so dense that they are ignorant of their own secrets, with strange creatures running across the landscape. For the world will never become old and grey. *You* humans become old and grey. As long as children are put into the world, the world is as new as on the seventh day when the Lord rested.'

Cecilia was open-mouthed, and the angel Ariel continued:

'Adam and Eve weren't the only people to be created. You are created a little as well. One day it was suddenly your turn to see what the Lord had done. You were shaken out of God's jacket sleeve and you found yourself in the air, all alive, alive-oh! And you saw that everything was extremely good.'

Cecilia couldn't help laughing. She asked, 'Have all of you really been here the whole time?'

The angel Ariel nodded solemnly.

'Here and there, yes. But we're just as curious about everything that has to do with the creation as we were half an eternity ago. And why shouldn't we be, for *we* view it all from the outside. Within creation only the children are as inquisitive as we are. But in a way they, too, come from outside.'

While Cecilia had been ill she had often thought the same: grown-ups always had to think before they decided to do anything that was fun. Nothing really surprised them, either. 'That's how things *are*, Cecilia,' they said.

'God must be fond of the grown-ups as well, mustn't he?' she suggested.

'Of course. Although they've all become a bit frayed around the edges since the Fall.'

'Frayed around the edges?'

'They've made the whole world a habit. It's not a habit for the angels in heaven, although we've existed through all eternity. We're still just as amazed at what God has created. Besides, he's quite astonished himself. That's why he takes more delight in inquisitive little children than in bothering about grown-ups' worldly-wise behaviour.'

Cecilia thought and thought until she felt as if sparks

were coming out of her head. This had happened to her many times before. While she had been ill her head had several times seemed like a whole funfair of clever thoughts. The only difference was that she didn't need to buy a ticket to get on any of the switchback rides.

'Most grown-ups have usually become so at home in the world that they take the whole of creation for granted,' Ariel commented. 'It's rather comical, when you think about it, because they're only here on a brief visit.'

'I agree with you.'

'We're talking about the world, Cecilia! As if the world were not a sensation! Maybe heaven ought to put an advertisement into the biggest newspapers at regular intervals: "Important announcement to all citizens of the world! It's not just a rumour: THE WORLD IS HERE NOW!"'

Cecilia felt giddy from listening to the angel Ariel. She felt giddy from watching him swinging and kicking his bare legs. 'Wouldn't it have been better,' she said, 'if God had driven that horrid serpent out of Paradise, so that Adam and Eve could have played hide-and-seek in the big garden for ever?'

The angel Ariel put his head on one side and said, 'It wasn't so easy. Because you are made of flesh and blood, you can't live for ever like the angels in heaven. But God didn't have the heart to let it be a part of creation that children had to die. It was better to let them grow up first.'

'Why?'

'It's much easier to say goodbye to the world when you've had half a dozen grandchildren and have grown a little tired and sleepy and full of days.'

Cecilia was not so impressed with this.

'Children do die sometimes,' she objected. 'Isn't that dumb?'

' "Isn't that dumb?" ' repeated the angel Ariel. ' "Isn't that dumb?" '

Since he didn't say anything else, Cecilia spoke again.

'Are you quite sure Adam and Eve were children?'

'Yes, quite sure. Has it never occurred to you that it's the children who look most like the angels in heaven? Or have you ever seen an angel with grey hair, a bad back, and a wrinkled face?'

There was something about this question that roused Cecilia to protest.

'I don't think that Grandma is ugly even though she *is* old.'

' "That Grandma is ugly",' repeated Ariel. 'We didn't say that. But inside her old body there lives a little Eve who was once quite new in the world. The rest is only something that has gradually grown on the outside as the years have passed.'

Cecilia sighed heavily.

'If I'm allowed to say what I think, I think the whole business of creation is pretty idiotic.'

'Why?'

'I don't ever want to grow up. I'm never going to die, so there! Never!'

A shadow fell across the angel's face. He said, 'You must try not to lose touch with the little child inside you. Grandma hasn't. She can even put on a clown's face now and again, just to get you to laugh, can't she?'

'Were you here then, too?'

'Yup!'

T HE next moment the angel Ariel was on the floor. Cecilia hadn't seen him jump down from the desk; he was simply standing in front of the bookcase all of a sudden, looking at all the crystals and precious stones. He was a little bit smaller than Lars.

'That's an impressive collection,' he said, with his back to her.

Then he turned round.

'Has it struck you that every single stone is a fragment of the earth?'

'Many times. I collect only the prettiest pieces.'

'But maybe it hasn't struck you that *you've* loosened your grip on the earth as well.'

She was surprised.

'Why?'

'You run about in creation on light feet. That's more than a stone can do.'

Only now was Cecilia able to see his face clearly. It was much smoother and purer than human skin; a little paler too. She had begun to get used to his having no hair on his head. Now she saw that he had no eyelashes or eyebrows either.

He walked towards her and sat down on the chair beside her bed. His footsteps were so light that it looked as if his feet were scarcely touching the floor; it was as if he was gliding across the room. His eyes shone like two turquoise gems, and when he smiled at her, as he did now, his teeth glittered like pieces of white marble.

Cecilia had stared at his shining head while they were talking. Now she said, 'Do you mind if I ask about your hair?'

He laughed. 'No. Just go ahead and ask. Then perhaps we can talk about your beard afterwards.'

She hid her face in the duvet.

'I thought angels had long, fair hair.'

'That's because you see everything in a looking-glass, so you can hardly avoid seeing yourself.'

She wasn't entirely satisfied with his answer.

'Can't you just tell me why angels have no hair on their heads?'

He said, 'Skin and hair grow on the body and fall off again all the time. They are connected with flesh and blood and act as protection against dust and dirt, cold and heat. Skin and hair are related to animal fur and have nothing to do with angels. You might just as well have asked whether we clean our teeth — or whether we cut our nails every other Saturday.'

'Because I suppose you don't do either of those things?'

He shook his head. 'It's not those things that make you and me similar.'

'What does, then?'

He looked down at her. 'Angels and humans both have a soul which is created by God. But humans have a body as well, which goes its own way. You grow and develop just like plants and animals.'

'Stupid,' sighed Cecilia. 'I don't like to think that I'm an animal.'

Ariel went on talking as if he hadn't heard what she said.

'All plants and animals begin their lives as tiny seeds or cells. At first they are so alike that you can't see any difference between them. But then the tiny seeds unfold slowly and turn into all sorts of things from redcurrant bushes and plumtrees to humans and giraffes. It takes a good many days before you can see the difference between a pig's embryo and a human embryo. Did you know that?'

She nodded. 'During the past weeks I've done hardly anything except read *Science Illustrated*.'

'And yet no humans are exactly alike, and no pigs either. Not even two blades of grass are identical in the whole of creation.'

Cecilia was suddenly reminded of a bag of Japanese magic balls that Father had given her many years ago. They had been so small that she couldn't tell them apart. But as soon as she put them in water they swelled up and turned into different shapes in all sorts of colours. Not one of them had resembled any of the others.

'I said I don't like to think that I'm an animal,' she repeated.

Ariel put his hand cautiously on the duvet. She could only just feel a light pressure against her leg.

'You are an animal with the soul of an angel, Cecilia. In that way you've been given the best of both worlds. Doesn't that sound fine?'

'I'm not sure . . .'

'It's precisely this combination which is such a great achievement. You're fully conscious, just like the angels in heaven: "Good evening, young man! My name is Cecilia Skotbu. May I have the next dance?"'

The angel Ariel extended one arm and bowed low. He looked as if he had come straight from dancing class. He went on:

'But the body you're living in is made of flesh and blood just like those of cows and camels. That's why hair grows on your body, mostly on your head of course, but it grows in other places as well, though there's only a very little to begin with. It grows quicker and quicker, Cecilia, more and more intensely as time passes! Nature grows like a thicker and thicker layer round the little child who has come into the world. When humans are released from the hand of the Creator their bodies are just as pure and smooth as those of the angels in heaven. But that's only on the outside, for the fall into sin is already taking place. Inside the body all

35

that flesh and blood is rampaging around, which means that you don't live for ever.'

Cecilia bit her lip. She didn't like talking about things to do with her body. She didn't like the idea that she had begun to grow up either.

'Little Lars didn't have a hair on his head until he was two,' she said.

'You don't need to tell me that.'

'Then perhaps you know that I was given some strong medicines at the hospital. They made my hair fall out.'

He nodded. 'Then we looked even more like each other.'

'I ought really to have had the same treatment again, but we changed our minds . . .'

'I know that too.'

'It was Grandma who persuaded them all, even the doctors. She's incredible when she gets going. So we just packed my bag and came home from the hospital. But Christmas comes several times a week. She's a nurse . . .'

'I know all about it.'

Cecilia looked up at the ceiling. For a while she lay thinking about everything that had happened during the past months. Then she turned towards Ariel again.

'Are you quite sure you're a proper angel?'

'I said angels never tell lies.'

'But if you *are* lying, you're not an angel, so you might be lying all the same.'

He sighed deeply. 'Oh, how complicated this suspiciousness of yours is!'

Cecilia felt a shiver go through her. Could it have been because she was so suspicious?

'May I ask you a typically stupid question?' she said.

'It's never stupid to ask questions.'

She took a deep breath.

'Are you a girl or a boy?'

Ariel laughed a clear ripple of laughter. It reminded Cecilia of the sound she made once when she had played on bottles filled with water. It was such fun to hear it that she repeated:

'Are you a girl or a boy?'

He must have seen through the question, because he laughed a little bit longer before he answered, and this time his laughter was rather strained.

'That was a *very* down-to-earth question.'

She felt insulted. Hadn't he just said it was never stupid to ask questions?

'Such peculiar differences don't exist in heaven,' he assured her. 'But I don't mind if you call me a "boy", then we'll be one of each kind.'

'Why are there such "peculiar differences" here, then?'

'We've talked about that already. There *have* to be two different sexes so that new children shall come into the world. You know that, Cecilia. Actually, it's not very interesting for an angel to talk about things like that.'

'Sorry!'

'No, that's all right. I'm sure God wouldn't have created any differences between boys and girls if they were not to become men and women and make new children. At the time, maybe he couldn't think of any other way of doing it. Have you a better suggestion?'

'I don't know.'

Now he became enthusiastic.

'If humans had come about through budding on a branch, you'd have been bound to ask why. But however anything *does* come about, everything *could* have been quite different. You might, for instance, have lived inside the planet instead of crawling around on the outside. It would probably have been possible to build towns and farms inside a planet, as long as the conditions were right. And if the conditions were not right, people would only have had to make an effort to get them right. Of course it's quite an achievement to create a whole world, but at least you start out with a clean sheet.'

'It's a crazy idea,' said Cecilia. 'And it gets crazier the more I think about it.'

'What is?'

'The idea that there are two kinds of humans on earth.'

He sat with a mischievous smile on his face.

'It's one of the things we discuss all the time in heaven. But it's not the same.'

'Why not?'

'Because we're discussing something that's different from ourselves. It must be even more strange to think it's odd to be what you are. I don't think you'd find a stone that thinks it odd to be a stone. And I'm certain no tortoise thinks it's remarkable to be a tortoise either. But certain humans apparently think it's strange to be a human. And I'm totally in agreement with them. I've never felt on the same wavelength with stones or tortoises.'

'Don't you think it's strange to be an angel?'

It took some time for him to answer.

'That's quite different, because that's what I've been through all eternity. You've been Cecilia Skotbu for only a short while.'

'Right! And I still consider that it's very strange to be me.'

'The whole creation is a puzzle, of course,' decided Ariel. 'All the same, the strangest thing of all is that on a few fringes of the great puzzle there are some beings who experience themselves as a puzzle.'

'Why is that so strange?'

'It's a bit as if a well were able to dive down into its own mysterious depths.'

'I've done that lots of times,' Cecilia assured him.

'What have you done?'

'I've stood in front of the mirror and looked myself in the eyes. Then I've imagined I'm a well that's so deep, it can't manage to stare down into its deepest depths.'

'That's because you're changing all the time. When you're gradually becoming different, you're bound to be a little surprised about it. If a caterpillar could think, I'm sure it would be very surprised when it suddenly realised it had turned into a butterfly. Things like that can happen almost overnight. But the angels in heaven are just as astonished when a little girl suddenly turns into a grown woman. That small difference in time doesn't mean so very much to us.'

'Why not?'

'Angels have plenty of time, Cecilia, and there's a very big difference between a little girl and a grown woman.'

'Is it true that you talk about such things in heaven?'

Ariel nodded shyly. He glanced round the room. Then he said, 'But we try not to do it when God's around. He's *very* sensitive to criticism.'

'I'd never have believed it.'

'But you believe so many things. You can't expect to have the same outlook as the angels in heaven.'

'I mean that I thought God was above all criticism.'

'Well, you've never met him face to face. But if you had created a whole world yourself, I'm sure you'd have been a little sensitive to criticism as well. We're talking about enormously important matters. Even though God looked out over all that he had created and thought it was exceedingly good, that doesn't mean he might not have done it differently. When he had finished creating it all he was so exhausted that he had to rest on the seventh day. He just collapsed, you see. I think it will be a very long time before he tries it again.'

Cecilia had enough to do, dealing with her own thoughts.

'Supposing there was only one sex,' she said, 'or three for that matter: perhaps that would have been best of all.'

'Don't you think men and women manage to create enough fuss and palaver as it is?'

'There can be a lot of fuss because there are no more than two sexes, after all, especially when a family has lots of children. It doesn't sound as if you know much about life on earth.'

Ariel shrugged.

'I'd like to learn more.'

'If it was necessary to have three sexes in order that children should be born,' insisted Cecilia, 'there might not have been quite so many, and in the first place that would have helped the problem of over-population – '

'Wait a bit,' protested the angel Ariel. 'You're going too fast for me.'

Cecilia sighed with impatience.

'I thought angels were quick on the uptake.'

'Not when you talk about childbirth and that sort of thing. Then we're as far away from heaven as it's possible for an angel to travel.'

'I only mean that it takes more effort for three people to like each other so much that they would want to have children together, than it does for only two people to

41

fall for each other head over heels, and then make children before they're perhaps sufficiently grown-up.'

'Pure mathematics, then. Because the two sexes who want to make children wouldn't be able to manage it without the help of the third sex. Is that all you mean?'

She nodded.

'If two of the three wanted to make children, perhaps the third would say, "No, folks. One of us must have some common sense. We ought to wait for a year or two. I'm not going to take part in making more children right now. It'll keep us far too busy." '

She couldn't help laughing at her own argument, and the laughter was catching, for Ariel joined in too.

'We wonder about interesting ideas like that in heaven, too.'

But Cecilia had more on her mind.

'Besides, there would be more people to look after the children, when they got ill, for instance. Then two of the grown-ups could have some time to themselves while the third mother or father looked after the children. Then there would be more people who were fond of children too. There would be far more people who were fond of each other.'

Ariel's expression had become inscrutable. He might have been sitting with the same look on his face through all eternity.

'Are humans really only fond of each other in their families?' he asked.

'Perhaps not, but I'm sure there would be more love

in the world if there were three or four parents. It's just that . . .'

'What?'

' . . . there would be more sadness as well.'

'Sadness?'

Cecilia bit her lip again. Then she said, 'When somebody died, there would be even more people to grieve.'

Ariel merely shook his head.

'I think you're going too fast again.'

'Why?'

'If it was like that, there would be twice as much comfort in the world too.'

'So perhaps it would all even out?'

He nodded. 'But if every family had only two children, there would be no humans left on earth in the end.'

'Why not?'

'If three grown-ups had only two children, there would gradually be fewer and fewer people. Finally it would all come to an end.'

Cecilia laughed. 'One fine day there would only be one Adam and one Eve left, just as when it began. As long as they were forgiven their original sin they could live in Paradise for ever. Wouldn't that be clever?'

'Not bad. But now we're discussing the creation itself.'

'And there's no point in that? You're talking almost like Mother. There's no "point" in grumbling about being ill, she says. But we can't be bothered to talk any more about illness and that sort of thing.'

'*I* didn't say anything about illness. But I promise to mention the three sexes next time I'm chatting with God. He has a sense of humour, after all.'

'Does he?'

He smiled indulgently.

'Have you ever seen an elephant? You have no idea how many elephant jokes we have in heaven. We have a number of giraffe jokes as well.'

Cecilia wasn't sure whether she liked the idea of the angels in heaven telling each other jokes about the creation. It seemed a bit flippant.

'I hope you don't tell any jokes about me,' she said.

'No, no. I've never heard so much as a single Cecilia joke. But even though you understand only in part, I'm sure you realise that it's too late to alter the system of creation now.'

'Perhaps – '

'Shall I tell you a secret?'

'Yes, please!'

'Sometimes when we talk about how everything is and how everything might have been, God throws up his arms in despair and says, "I know that plenty of things might have been a little different, but what's done is done, and I'm not almighty, after all."'

Cecilia's jaw dropped. 'You won't find a single priest to agree with you about that.'

'In that case, either the priests or God are mistaken.'

Cecilia put a hand to her mouth and gasped. At the same time a frown passed over the angel's face.

'Your mother's coming,' he said. 'I'll have to hurry.'

'I can't hear anything.'

'But she *is* coming.'

Cecilia heard the alarm clock ringing in the next room.

'Are you going away?'

He shook his head. 'I'll sit on the windowsill.'

'Can't Mother see you?'

'I don't think so.'

The next moment Cecilia's mother came in.

'Cecilia?'

'Mmm . . .'

'Have you got the light on?'

'You can see I have.'

'I just wanted to find out how you were.'

'Is it morning?'

'It's three o'clock.'

'But I heard the alarm.'

'I set it for three.'

'Why did you do that?'

'Because I love you. I can't leave you alone for a whole night, not a whole Christmas night, at any rate.'

'Go back to sleep again, Mother.'

'Will you be able to sleep?'

'Sometimes I sleep, sometimes I lie awake. I can't separate the two.'

'Is there anything you want?'

'I have water.'

'And you don't want to go to the bathroom?'

She shook her head.

'It was lovely when you sang. I fell asleep even though Grandma was playing the piano.'

'Shall I air the room a little?'

'Maybe a little.'

Mother went to the window. Cecilia thought she could see Ariel on the windowsill, but he faded more and more as Mother went nearer.

'Do you see that there are ice roses on the pane?' she asked. 'Isn't it strange how they manage to draw themselves?'

She opened the window.

'Lots of things are strange, Mother. But it's as if I understand everything so much better now that I'm ill. It's as if the whole world has become a little clearer at the edges.'

'It's often like that. All we need is a bad dose of influenza to hear the birds outside in quite a different way.'

'Did I tell you that the postman waved to me?'

'Yes, you did. There – now I'll shut it again.'

She went back to the bed and gave Cecilia a hug.

'Sleep well, then. I'll set the alarm for seven.'

'You don't need to. It's Christmas.'

'That's why. But Cecilia – '

'Yes?'

'Can't we move your bed into our room? It might be

more cosy for you . . . and a bit easier for Father and me.'

'Can't you come here instead?'

'Yes, of course we can. You must ring the bell as often as you like – even if it's in the middle of the night.'

'Yes, of course. But Mother . . .'

'Yes?'

'If I were God I'd have created the world so that all children had at least three parents.'

'Why do you say that?'

'Because then you wouldn't be so tired. And then you and Father could be on your own a bit while the third mother or father was with Little Lars and me.'

'You mustn't say things like that.'

'Why not? I know it's impossible to change the creation. It's just that sometimes I think God's a great big nitwit. He's not even almighty!'

'I think you're a bit angry inside yourself because you're ill.'

'A *bit*?'

'Very, then. Sleep well now. There's no point in being angry, Cecilia.'

' "There's no point in being angry, Cecilia." You've said that a hundred times already.'

'But I hope and pray that you'll get well again. We all do.'

'Of course I'll get well again. That's really one of the silliest things you've said for a long time.'

'Christine's coming tomorrow to give you your injection.'

'There, you see!'

'What?'

'You surely don't think she'd bother to come all that long way on Christmas Day unless she thought the medicine would help. You're nuts, Mother. Your brain's gone sloppy because you've lived far too long.'

'Of course she thinks the medicine helps. I do too . . . Are you sure you don't want to move in with us?'

'I shall soon be grown-up! Don't you realise that's why I want my own room?'

'Yes, of course I do.'

'No fun to lie awake listening to both of you snoring either.'

'I realise that too.'

'But you mustn't take it personally . . . Thank you for my presents, by the way.'

'Shall I turn off the light?'

'No, I'll do it myself. I'll do it as soon as I've finished thinking.'

W HEN Mother had gone back to her room Cecilia fished for her pen and notebook on the floor under the bed. She wrote:

Every single second some brand-new children are shaken out of the sleeve of nature's jacket. Hocus pocus! Every single second many people disappear too. O U T spells out, and out Cecilia must go . . .

It's not we who come into the world, but the world that comes to us. To be born is the same as to be given the whole world as a gift.

Sometimes God throws up his arms in despair and says to himself: 'I know that plenty of things might have been a little different, but what's done is done, and I'm not almighty, after all.'

Cecilia pushed the book and the pen in under the bed, and dropped off again.

She didn't know how much time had passed when she opened her eyes and looked up. The light from the big tree in the garden was pouring into the room. The ice roses on the window pane looked like gold.

'Ariel,' she whispered.

'I'm here.'

'But I can't see you.'

'Here . . .'

Now she saw him. He had made himself comfortable on top of the bookshelf where there were no books.

'How did you manage to get up there?'

'That's no problem for an angel. Have you slept well?'

The next moment he was on the floor. Cecilia hadn't seen him jump down, nor had she heard any sound. All of a sudden there he was, down on the floor, touching her new skis.

'Splendid skis!' he said. 'Splendid toboggan too!'

He turned towards her, and she saw again how beautiful he was. His eyes were even clearer than she remembered, green and full of secrets. Cecilia thought they reminded her of a certain precious stone; there was a good picture of it in the big book about gemstones. Wasn't its name the star sapphire?

'How did you know Mother was coming?' she asked.

' "Mother was coming",' repeated Ariel. ' "How did you know Mother was coming?".'

'Copycat!'

'I'm only tasting the words.'

'*Tasting* the words?'

He nodded. 'In fact that's the only thing an angel *can* taste.'

'Did they taste good, then?'

'A bit strange too.'

'Why?'

'Don't you think it's the slightest bit strange that once upon a time you were lying splashing inside her stomach?'

Cecilia sighed indulgently. She remembered that matters to do with the birth of babies were the furthest point an angel could go from heaven.

'How did you know she was coming?' she asked.

'She had set the clock for three.'

'You surely can't see through walls as well?'

He took a step towards her.

'It's time you gave up this nonsense. What you call "walls" are not walls to us.'

She put a hand to her mouth.

'Then you have X-ray eyes. Can you see through my body?'

'If I decide I want to. But I don't know how it *feels* when all that food you humans eat churns round in your stomachs and turns into flesh and blood.'

She shuddered. 'I think we should talk about something else.'

'Suits me.'

'Can you come a little closer?'

The next moment he was sitting on the chair beside the bed. It was as if he had only changed places without crossing the floor, almost the way an image moves about the room as one turns the slide-projector.

'I couldn't see you moving,' she said. 'Suddenly you were sitting here.'

'We don't need to "move" the way you do. Just tell me where you want me to go and I'm there in an instant.'

'You must explain that to me. And then you must tell me how you manage to go through closed doors, for that's something I've never understood.'

He hesitated. 'I'll do it on one condition.'

Cecilia was surprised. 'I didn't know angels laid down conditions for their good deeds.'

'But you're not asking me to do a good deed. You're asking me to give away heavenly secrets.'

'What are the conditions, then?'

'That you tell me about earthly secrets.'

'Poof, you know everything.'

Ariel sat on the edge of the chair.

'I don't know how it feels to have a body of flesh and blood. I don't know how it feels to grow. I don't know how it feels to eat, to be cold, or to dream sweet dreams.'

'I'm sure I'm not the first person you've spoken to. Didn't you say you've all existed for ever?'

'I also said that angels never cease to be amazed at the creation. And we don't reveal ourselves so very often. The last time I was on angel watch was in Germany more than a hundred years ago.'

'Who were you sitting with then?'

'His name was Albert, and he was very ill.'

'How did it turn out for him?'

'Not so well, unfortunately. That was why I was there.'

Cecilia snorted. 'I don't suppose you come visiting only when things go wrong. That's one of the silliest things I ever heard.'

'It's never silly to comfort someone who's upset.'

'Didn't *he* tell you what it's like to be a human made of flesh and blood?'

Ariel shook his head. 'He was far too small.'

'That's a pity.'

'Why?'

'Because I sort of have to do the whole job myself.'

'But you'll go along with the agreement?'

Cecilia tried to work herself a little higher up in bed.

'I'll try,' she said. 'But you must begin.'

'Agreed!'

He settled himself comfortably. Two bare legs stuck out from under the white tunic. He slung them over on to Cecilia's bed. His legs were as smooth as those of a newborn child. Cecilia couldn't see so much as a pore in his skin.

Before she met Ariel she had never thought that body hair had anything to do with plants and animals. Now she understood how strange it would have been if an angel had had hair on his legs. All sorts of things could sprout and grow on old trees. On humans and animals too. Moss and lichen could even grow on stones. But nothing could grow on an angel.

She noticed his toenails. It was clear that they never needed cutting. They, too, reminded her of one of her stones. Was it the one called rock crystal?

'Do angels get tired?' she asked.

'Why should you think they do?'

'You put your feet up on the bed.'

He smiled warmly. 'I've seen how humans sit when they're going to have a heart-to-heart talk.'

'Copycat again! Why can't you be yourself? Mother usually says, "Don't be shy".'

'Then maybe I can ask you to sit up in the bed? It's a bit of a nuisance after a time having to talk to someone who's just lolling about.'

'I'm *rather* ill, you know.'

'Just pull yourself up, Cecilia.'

She tried to do as the angel said, and soon they were sitting feet to feet: Cecilia in bed, Ariel on the chair. Cecilia felt much better. It was a long time since she had sat up with her back straight. She began to think what she should tell the angel about earthly secrets.

Ariel began.

'Many humans believe that an angel is a ghost that flaps around between heaven and earth without a proper body – '

'That's just how I've imagined angels myself.'

54

'But it's the opposite. To us you're the ones who are light and airy. When you kick a stone, your foot hits the stone. If I did the same, I'd simply kick straight through it. It's no more solid to me than a piece of fog.'

'Then I understand how you can glide through doors and windows without hurting yourselves. But I don't understand why the walls aren't spoiled.'

'When you walk in fog, the fog isn't spoiled either. And when you think about something, your thoughts can't do any harm to the world about you.'

'That may be. But if you can dive through a wall it must be because you don't have a proper body.'

'Feel my foot, Cecilia.'

She put two fingers round his big toe and squeezed. It was like touching a piece of steel.

Ariel said, 'We have much more solid bodies than anything in creation. An angel can never be destroyed. That's because we don't have a body of flesh and blood that our souls can be parted from.'

'You can be glad of that.'

'But nature isn't like that. Here everything is destroyed very easily. Even a mountain is slowly ground down by the forces of nature and turns to earth and sand in the end.'

'Thank you for the information, but I know all about that.'

'You are ghosts to us, Cecilia, not the other way round. You come and go. You are the ones who don't last. You suddenly appear, and each time a newborn child is laid on its mother's stomach, it's just as wonderful. But just as suddenly you've gone. It's as if God is blowing bubbles with you.'

Cecilia screwed up her eyes.

'Excuse me for saying so directly, but that seems a bit suspicious.'

He nodded. 'That's probably quite a good way of putting it. There's mischief afoot in nature. There's trouble brewing in creation.'

'I don't think it's particularly comfortable to be trouble brewing. I don't like the idea of being a "ghost" either.'

Ariel had put a hand to his mouth — as if he suddenly realised he had said too much.

'But you're not ghosts to one another,' he hastened to add. 'Doesn't your father have to take a good grip on you and flex all his muscles every time he carries you down into the living room?'

'Blah, blah!'

'Why do you say that?'

'You have such clever answers to everything I ask you about. But I haven't observed that any of the things you've said are true.'

'So there we are again!'

'Where?'

'You still think I'm telling lies.'

She pretended she hadn't heard.

'For instance, can you walk through the wall to Mother and Father to see whether they're asleep?'

'We're not supposed to play too many games like that.'

'Just once, then?'

Ariel got up from the chair and walked slowly across the floor. When he reached the wall he went on walking. Cecilia watched him glide through the wall. Finally only one foot was left, then that too was drawn into the wall and vanished. A few seconds later the opposite happened. Ariel slid slowly out of the wall and stood in the middle of the room.

'They're both asleep,' he said. 'He has put an arm across her shoulder. The alarm clock is set for seven.'

'Bravo!' exclaimed Cecilia, clapping her hands. 'So I *don't* need to sleep in Mother's and Father's room.'

'No. If you want anything, I can wake them quicker than any alarm clock.'

'Is that true?'

He smiled a resigned smile. It must have been because she didn't believe him again.

He said, 'It's just as much fun every time. They think they wake up on their own. Then they say, "Wasn't it strange that I should wake just then? I had a feeling something was wrong."'

'It was fun to see you do it.'

'It's fun to watch grown-ups when they're asleep too. They often look like little children. Perhaps they're dreaming that they're outside, playing in the snow.'

Cecilia brightened. 'You've given me an idea! Can't you creep down to the hall and fetch me a snowball? You don't even need to unlock the door.'

Ariel had already got up from the chair.

'All I need to do is put my hand through the window pane,' he said. 'There's plenty of snow on the window ledge outside.'

And that's what he did. He jumped up on to the writing desk and Cecilia could see how he pushed his arm right through the closed window. The next moment he was back in the room with a small snowball in his hand. The window pane remained whole.

She stared. 'Super!'

'Are you satisfied now?'

'Not quite. I'd like to feel the snow myself.'

'Here you are,' said Ariel, and threw the snowball on to Cecilia's duvet. She took it in her hands.

'Ice-cold,' she said. 'It's the first time I've felt this year's snow.'

'"This year's snow",' repeated Ariel. 'It almost sounds like "this season's fruit" or "the harvest of the sea".'

Cecilia had put the snowball against her cheek. When it began dripping she dropped it into the glass on her bedside table. Ariel sat down again.

'I've never felt the snow myself,' he said, almost as if he were sulking. 'I know I'll never be able to. Not for all eternity.'

'You must be joking! You've just felt it.'

'I didn't feel anything. Angels don't *feel* anything, Cecilia.'

'Didn't you feel that it was cold?'

He had a resigned expression.

'You really must learn these things. If you don't, it won't be much fun talking to you. Feeling a snowball is the same for us as feeling a thought. *You* can't feel the memory of the snow that fell last year.'

She shook her head, and Ariel asked, 'How does it feel to hold a snowball?'

'Cold – ice-cold.'

'You've said that already.'

Now she had to try hard.

'Your skin prickles. It tingles like strong peppermints. You want to take your hand away and shiver. But it's lovely all the same.'

Ariel had leaned over her inquisitively as she spoke.

'I've never tasted peppermint,' he said. 'I've never shivered either.'

Only now did Cecilia begin to see that it was as difficult for Ariel to understand earthly things as it had been for her to understand heavenly things.

She said, 'It must be horrid to touch something without feeling it. One of the worst things I know is an anaesthetic at the dentist's.'

' "An anaesthetic at the dentist's",' he repeated.

'But it must be even worse to be completely anaesthetised. You can't even feel you're alive then.'

His expression was inscrutable. Then he asked, 'Can you feel all over your body?'

Cecilia laughed. 'Not in my hair. Not in my nails either.'

'But everywhere where you have skin, and that's almost everywhere. The flesh and blood are sealed inside a magic suit which helps you to feel all your surroundings. Imagine it being possible to create something like that!'

'A magic suit?'

'Your skin, Cecilia. I mean this fine-meshed web of nerves. When God created the world he did it in such a clever way that the creation was able to feel itself. Don't you agree that it was clever?'

'Maybe . . .'

'Are you equally sensitive all over your body?'

She had to think for a bit.

'I'm not equally ticklish everywhere. In some places it's specially good to be tickled. Sometimes it can be so nice it almost hurts. Did you know that something can be so nice it almost hurts?'

' "Did you know that something can be so nice it almost hurts?" '

'Now you're being a copycat again.'

Ariel shook his bald head.

'I'm only trying to understand what you say. Can anything hurt so much it's almost nice, too?'

'No.'

'You must excuse my asking. You see, angels don't know exactly what pain is.'

'Are you really as unfeeling as earth and stone?'

He nodded solemnly. 'At least!'

'I don't know which I'd prefer.'

'To be a stone or an angel?'

'I mean that if I had no feelings I'd never have felt pain either. To be completely anaesthetised would perhaps be best.'

'Then maybe it's the dentist you don't much like, and not the anaesthetic.'

She nodded.

'But I think it's a bit worrying that the angels in heaven don't know the difference between what feels good and what hurts.'

Again she was about to say that she wasn't quite sure whether she believed in angels. Then she had a sudden inspiration.

'Why don't you have wings?'

He laughed. ' "Angels' wings" are only an old super-stition that began when people thought the world was flat as a pancake and that the angels flew up and down between heaven and earth all the time. It's not quite so simple.'

'How is it, then?'

'Birds needs wings to take flight because they're made of flesh and blood. We're made of spirit, so we don't need wings to move about the creation.'

She smiled. 'That's the same as it is with my thoughts. They don't need wings either to flutter about the world.'

Before she had finished talking Ariel rose from the chair and began hovering about the room like an air balloon. Cecilia watched him.

'Super!' she exclaimed. 'Doesn't *that* feel wonderful?'

He alighted in front of the bookcase.

'I don't feel anything.'

'That must be a strange feeling. It must be a strange feeling not to feel anything.'

'But your thoughts can't feel what they're thinking, the way you can feel a snowball in your hand.'

He picked up the new skis and held them up to her.

'Is it nice to go skiing?'

Cecilia nodded. 'I'm going to try them out soon.'

'But it must be a typically "cold" experience, especially when you fall into the snow. Do you get that shivering taste of strong peppermint all over?'

'Not if we have enough clothes on. Then all we feel is that the snow is as soft as cotton wool. Sometimes we take off our skis and print angels in the snow. That's fun!'

Ariel had replaced the skis. He said, 'We really appreciate that. Besides, it shows how closely related human children are to God's children in heaven.'

'Does it really?'

He nodded solemnly. 'In the first place, because you make angels. You could easily have made something quite different. In the second place, because you have such fun. All angels like doing fun things.'

'Don't you think grown-ups like doing fun things too?'

Ariel shrugged. 'Have you ever seen a grown-up skier take off his skis and lie down flat in deep snow to make angels?'

She nodded. 'Once Grandma did exactly that.'

'There, you see!'

'What?'

'*She* hasn't lost contact with the child inside her.'

Ariel started hovering about the room again. When he landed on the chair beside Cecilia's bed he said, 'I'm sorry to have to say so, but this is getting a bit dull.'

'What is?'

He sighed resignedly. 'This is a rare meeting between heaven and earth. I was supposed to tell you a great many things about the secrets of heaven if *you* told *me* how it feels to be made of flesh and blood.'

Cecilia felt limp and exhausted because she considered that the angel Ariel had begun repeating himself. She said, 'It is a bit dull, just lying here.'

He nodded. 'So far this angel watch hasn't exactly been the most fun.'

'Shall we go down to the living room? I was there only while they handed out the presents.'

' "Shall we go down to the living room?" ' repeated Ariel. 'Yes, why not? It's still Christmas night.'

'Do you think you can help me downstairs?'

'Of course.'

'Can you manage to lift me?'
'You don't weigh anything to us, Cecilia.'
'Carry me down, then!'

ARIEL put his outstretched arm under Cecilia and lifted her from the bed. It felt quite different from being lifted by Father. He usually puffed and panted and made heavy weather of it. On the angel's arm Cecilia felt as light as a feather, even though he was much smaller than she was.

They crept out into the passage and down the stairs to the ground floor. There was no Grandad smoking cigars in the hall. But would he have seen the angel Ariel if he *had* been there? Or would he have thought Cecilia was hovering in thin air?

The living room was almost completely dark. Only the lamp above the green wing chair had been left on.

'They usually put me on the sofa,' she said.

He lowered her carefully on to the red sofa, and Cecilia looked up.

'They've turned off the tree lights. What a shame!'

The next moment Ariel had put the plug into the socket. He stood in front of the tree and threw out his arms. The lights on the tree filled the room with a Christmas feeling.

'That was quick,' she said. 'You remind me of a genie of the lamp, who fulfils every wish. Do you see how beautiful the tree is?'

He nodded solemnly. 'It looks like the lights in heaven.'

'Does it? I've often wondered. Do they decorate with cotton wool there too?'

'The lights of heaven are all the stars and the planets,' he explained. 'There are different gases round some of the planets. Don't you think that may be why you use cotton wool round the tree lights?'

'I've never thought about it. But every single Christmas we argue about whether we should have cotton wool on the Christmas tree. Mother hates it, and so does Grandma, but this year they didn't dare contradict me.'

'At least you have *one* star right at the top.'

She looked up. 'The one we had before vanished. But this one's a bit crooked.'

The next moment Ariel was hovering near the top of the Christmas tree. Cecilia watched him. They had hung a few paper angels on the tree, some of them white, some of them gold. Now there was a real angel flying round it!

'Is it straight now?'

'I think so. But don't come back to the floor yet. I love watching you.'

Ariel hovered just below the ceiling and lay seesawing a metre above the dining table.

'I wish I could fly,' she said. 'Then I might have run away from it all.'

He pointed at a large dish full of cakes and marzipan sweets.

'They haven't taken away the cake dish.'

'No. Please help yourself.'

Ariel circled above the dish. He said, 'It would have been fun if I could.'

'Of course you can. You've no idea how much they've been baking.'

He gave a deep sigh. 'I've told you, angels don't eat. We *can't* eat.'

'Oh! . . . I forgot.'

' "Time, like an ever-rolling stream, bears all its sons away." So, new tables are continually laid with different kinds of food and drinks. But the angels in heaven will never know what it's like to taste any earthly joys.'

'Could you please pass me a cookie?'

Ariel dived down and fetched her a cookie. He floated across the room and handed it to Cecilia, who began biting tiny pieces. He stayed hovering above the sofa.

'It's terribly funny to watch you humans eat,' he said.

'Why?'

'You put something in your mouth and smack your lips and chew away, and then it tastes of something or other before it turns into flesh and blood.'

'Yes, that's what happens.'

'How many different tastes are there?'

'No idea. I don't think anyone's ever made a proper list of tastes.'

'What do you think's the very best?'

She considered it thoroughly.

'Strawberries, maybe . . . strawberries and ice cream.'

He rolled his eyes. 'It sounds a bit odd to be putting those cold peppermint lumps in your mouth. You must feel things beginning to shiver and tickle inside you?'

'You make it sound so strange. But it's true that it sometimes does tickle right down in my stomach. Wonderful!'

Ariel went on hovering above the sofa. Now and again he backed away; then he would seesaw a little closer.

He pointed at the dining table. 'There are some strawberries in the dish there.'

She laughed. 'Those are only Lars's marzipan straw-berries.'

'Do they taste very different from other strawber-ries?'

'Yes, very different. But both of them could have been on the list of nice tastes.'

She looked up into the piercing sapphire eyes.

'Can you try to describe the difference between an ordinary strawberry and a marzipan strawberry?' he asked.

Cecilia was still chewing the cookie. She glanced at the dish with the marzipan strawberries, took a deep breath and said, 'A garden strawberry tastes sweet and sour – and red, of course. If you eat a marzipan strawberry, it also tastes red because we've used cochineal, but first and foremost it tastes of delicious dry-sweet marzipan.'

' "Delicious dry-sweet marzipan".'

'Did you know that marzipan is made of almonds? That's why I say dry-sweet, because the nuts are dry. The sweetness comes from the icing sugar.'

She licked a few crumbs from her hand.

'I don't really want either of them at the moment because I'm not well. But since it's Christmas, I feel I ought at least to think about it.'

Ariel shook his head in despair.

'I'm not much the wiser! Tastes and that kind of thing are unfathomable mysteries for the angels in heaven.'

'Not for God, surely, since he created everything?'

Ariel fluttered down and sat on her legs. He weighed nothing. He scarcely touched her; she didn't even feel a tickle.

'One doesn't always understand fully what one creates,' he said.

'Why not?'

'For instance, you can draw or paint something on a sheet of paper. But that doesn't mean you understand *how* it is to be whatever you've drawn.'

'That's quite different, because it's not alive.'

He nodded energetically. 'And that's precisely what's strange.'

'What is?'

'That humans are alive.'

Cecilia stared up at the ceiling.

'You're certainly right that God doesn't understand how stupid it is to be ill on Christmas Eve.'

He interrupted her. 'We can talk about God later. First you were going to tell me how it is to be a person of flesh and blood.'

'Ask me, then! Ask anything you want.'

'We've talked about how it is to taste something. It's just as strange that you can smell different things without your nose having to be close to what you're smelling. What *are* all these "smells" floating round in creation?'

'Perhaps you can't smell the Christmas tree either, can you?'

He sighed despondently. 'Angels have no senses, Cecilia. This isn't an exam in religious knowledge, but you must try to learn.'

'Sorry.'

'How does the tree smell?'

'Green . . . and then it smells acid and fresh . . . and a bit damp. But it smells sweet as well. I would say that the smell of the Christmas tree is almost half the Christmas feeling. Then come spicy cabbage and incense in second and third place. In fourth place come Grandad's cigars, but that can almost be too much of a good thing.'

'Can you smell the lights?'

'Not really, no.'

'Does that mean you don't quite agree with yourself?'

'The tree smells slightly different after we've decorated it and switched on the lights. Only a little, but that little extra is very important for the Christmas feeling.'

'Well, well. I don't think we'll get any further with the smells than we did with the tastes. Is there an endless number of different smells too?'

'There may be, but I don't think humans have a very good sense of smell. Maybe we can smell a hundred different smells, while we can taste a thousand different tastes. Dogs have a much better sense of smell. I think they can tell the difference between thousands of smells. That's not so very surprising when you think that half a dog's face is one big nose.'

'You're not bad at explanations, after all. Can you tell me what it's like to see?'

'You can see, just the same as I can, surely?'

Ariel took off from the sofa, sailed through the room, and sat down in the green wing chair. He was so small by comparison with the big chair that it looked as if he might drown in it.

'I don't see things in the same way,' he said. 'And I'm not patched together out of earth and water, either. I'm not a piece of living plasticine.'

'How *do* you see, then?'

'You can call it a spiritual presence.'

'But you can *see* me?'

He shook his head. 'I'm simply here.'

'I am too. And we can see each other the whole time, can't we?'

He shrugged. 'Would you say that you can see when you dream?'

'I can often see very clearly in dreams.'

'But you don't see with your eyes.'

'No, because they're closed when I sleep.'

'So perhaps you can understand that there are several ways of seeing. Some people are blind. They have to use their inner eye. That's the same eye that you see with when you dream pleasant dreams.'

' "The inner eye"?'

He nodded.

'It's quite a different matter when you blink with your eyelids and use the living lenses to observe nature around you. If you peel an onion or get a bit of dust in your eye, your sight is irritated. In the worst case it can fail. But nothing can damage the inner eye.'

'Why not?'

'Because it isn't made of flesh and blood.'

'What is it made of, then?'

'Of mind and thought.'

'It sounds a bit creepy.'

He was resting his elbows on the arms of the chair. He looked even smaller in the deep chair.

72

He said, 'I think it's much more creepy that a pair of living eyes, made of atoms and molecules, can see everything in the same room. You can even look out into the universe and perceive a little of the glory of heaven. But what you see with are a couple of glassy lumps that are closely related to fish eyes.'

'Seeing becomes very mysterious when you describe it that way.'

He brushed this aside with a gesture of his hand.

'It doesn't become any more mysterious than it is already. Once, many millions of years ago, some of the fish in the sea got a couple of flippers with bones in them to walk with. So these small, amphibious creatures crawled up on land, and looked around to find something to eat. Now you can see thousands of light years out into the universe with the same eyes that once upon a time had no other stars to look at than starfish and sea urchins. And more than that: you can lie on a red sofa and look one of the angels of the Lord in the eye.'

She laughed. 'I agree with you. It *is* strange to think about it.'

'If God had not created sight, he would not have shared the creation with human beings. The Garden of Eden would have remained in pitch darkness.'

' "In pitch darkness", ' repeated Cecilia. It sounded so terribly sad.

'Every single eye is a tiny scrap of the divine mystery,' continued Ariel. 'Sight is the very meeting place of object and thought; it is the very gate of pearl between sun and mind. The human eye is the very glass in which the creative space in God's consciousness meets itself in the created space outside.'

She stopped him with a gesture.

'I don't think I understood the last things you said.'

And the angel Ariel explained:

'Some of the angels in heaven believe that every single eye that sees God's creation is God's own eye. For who has said that God does not have many billions of eyes? Perhaps he has scattered billions of small photocells over creation so that he can see what he has created from several billion different angles. Since humans can't swim many hundred yards under the sea, he has given the fishes eyes too. And humans can't fly, but at any given time a living carpet of birds' eyes is lying below the sky, peeping down at the earth. But this isn't all.'

'Tell me more, please!'

'Sometimes it happens that a human being lifts his eyes towards his heavenly origin. Then it's as if God sees himself in the mirror.'

She let out her breath. 'Sky and sea!' she exclaimed.

'Yes. Like the sky and the sea.'

'What then?'

'The sky mirrors itself in the sea. In that way God can mirror himself in a pair of human eyes. For the eye is the mirror of the soul, and God is able to mirror himself in a human soul.'

She was enormously impressed.

'You ought to have been a priest; unless that's all heresy, of course.'

He smiled mischievously. 'We're not so particular about such things in heaven. There we've always known that the creation is a great puzzle, and when something is a puzzle, you must be allowed to guess a bit too.'

She hunched her shoulders. 'When you're so serious I get shivers up and down my spine. Though I might have a slight fever as well. *Must* we talk about all these senses any more?'

'There are only two left. Are you fond of singing and music?'

'At the moment I like listening to Christmas carols. Before I met you, I always thought my favourite singer must look like an angel. But now I realise that her "angel hair" only shows that *she*'s descended from the apes too. Some people say I look like her, in fact.'

'Do they?'

'What do you think?'

'I can see a resemblance.'

'Have you seen her, then?'

'I could hardly have avoided it.'

'Which sense are we talking about now?'

Ariel laughed. 'It's great fun to talk to you, Cecilia. I asked whether you like music so that you should tell me how it is to hear something. The angels in heaven simply cannot understand that flesh and blood have been given that ability.'

'Is that so strange?'

'Don't you think it's a small mystery that birds can twitter so loudly that they can hear each other's song from several miles away? Those tiny bundles are like living flutes, playing non-stop on themselves. It's just as amazing that all the words I say can reach you.'

'I think you're exaggerating the difference between us again. You can hear what I say too.'

Ariel sighed loudly. 'If you compare us once more just to make it easier for yourself, I shall visit another patient instead. There are very many sick people who never get so much as one brief angel visit.'

She replied quickly. 'I'm sure you mean you can't hear with living ears like me, but that we sort of just mix our thoughts.'

'Something like that, yes. I'm sorry I said that about another patient, by the way. It's not your fault that you only understand in part. You see everything in a glass, darkly . . .'

' "In a glass, darkly . . ." '

'This time you were the copycat,' he said.

'I was only tasting the words!'

'Once the earth was deserted and empty,' concluded Ariel. 'Then it became able to hear its own sounds. For many millions of years there had been thunder and lightning, the sea had washed against the cliffs, and the volcanoes had tossed out their streams of lava with tremendous force. But nobody heard anything at all. Today this globe can hear its own sounds. Venus or Mars can't do that. And if it were to get too quiet, all you have to do is put on an organ concerto by Johann Sebastian Bach. I like big concerts out of doors the best. Then the planet's most beautiful sounds swell out into space. And then there are all the radio concerts. The globe plays its own music: a little musical top of an earth-globe spinning round a fiery sun in the Milky Way.'

'Perhaps you should have been a poet,' suggested Cecilia. 'As long as you're not too modern.'

'I'd rather have been a scholar in the natural sciences. Because I don't really understand what's going on when you talk to each other and the invisible words seem to creep out of a mouth and then crawl through a narrow ear before they finally fuse with a jelly-like lump of a brain.'

That's what happened now, just as the angel had described it. The strange words he had spoken fused with Cecilia's brain and became her own thoughts. She lay so long thinking about it that Ariel started talking again.

'It's equally strange how you manage to shape all the words in your mouths. Sometimes it goes tremendously fast, and it's as if the words pour out of their own accord. Do you sometimes not know exactly what you're saying until after you've said it?'

She dropped her gaze. 'We don't always think about everything we do. When I have to run to school, I just run. I haven't time to think about how I'm moving my legs. If I did, I'm sure I'd trip up. It's like that sometimes when we talk to each other. Sometimes we trip over the words.'

'Then you have to breathe in all the time – and breathe out again. Does that happen on its own too?'

'I think so.'

'It sounds a bit sinister. Because if you forgot to breathe in one single time, your heart would stop beating. And if your heart stopped beating – '

'Stop it!' interrupted Cecilia. 'Luckily that's not the only thing we need to think about.'

He put a hand to his mouth. 'Sorry! We were talking about how you shape all the invisible words in your mouths before they begin floating round between the mouth and the ear. Is it true that each voice is different?'

Cecilia nodded. 'It sounds quite different when Mother says "Have you slept well?" from when Father or Grandma says exactly the same. I can lie with my head under the bedclothes and know exactly who's talking to me. Every single word is spoken slightly differently by everyone. The same is true of musical instruments. It sounds quite different when a clarinet plays a middle C from when the same note is played on a violin. And I've read that no two violins have exactly the same resonance. That's how it is with our voices too.'

'Which shows what delicate instruments the voice and the ear are.'

'Even when the window is shut I can hear that the wind is blowing outside; or that the postman is coming along the road on his bicycle – oh, you should have seen him when he fell off!'

'I was sitting in the window just as you were.'

'You must be everywhere! When the house is completely quiet I can sometimes hear it snowing.'

She had begun waving her arms about.

'And then, I can *see* with my ears!'

'Nonsense!' The angel Ariel's expression was forbidding. 'Even though we're talking about very extraordinary things, you mustn't start teasing me.'

'But it's true! When I'm lying in my room listening to sounds from down below, I can sort of see what they're doing and how everything looks down there.'

'Then you've been given a little bit of angel sight.'

She pulled herself up on the sofa. 'I've thought all along that you exaggerate the difference between angels and humans.'

'It's even stranger, since we have very different backgrounds. Humans are forged out of a few million molecules on a chance planet in space, and you're here for only a short time. But you dance through creation on light feet. You chat and laugh and think clever thoughts just like the angels in heaven.'

'Don't you think it's just as strange to be an angel?'

'We've discussed that already. The difference is that we've been here all along. Besides, we know we'll never fall into the empty void like a spent soap bubble. We simply *are*, Cecilia. We are that which has always been and always shall be. You come and go.'

She sighed a big sigh. 'I wish I'd thought more about how it is to live.'

'It's never too late.'

'I don't quite know why, but I'm suddenly so sad.'

He tried to check her. 'Don't be sad. Because if you are I'll have to try to be sympathetic. Sometimes I have the impression that you humans do nothing but whimper and complain.'

'That's easy for you to say!'

'We have only one sense left. It's a bit vaguer, but it's no less puzzling because of that.'

She dried a tear. 'I don't remember what the fifth sense is called – feeling?'

He nodded. 'We've talked about the thin covering of skin and hair which all flesh and blood is wrapped in from top to toe. When you taste what you eat you do it with your tongue, but in a way you can taste with your whole body. You taste whether something is cold or hot, wet or dry, smooth or rough.'

'I don't think that's so surprising.'

'For an angel it's perhaps the most surprising of all. The stones at the edge of the sea can't feel that they're rattling against each other when the waves crash on the shore. A stone can't feel when you pick it up either. But *you* can feel the stone.'

'Have you looked at my stone collection properly? I've bought some of them, I've been given others, but most of them I've found on the beach. On an "unknown beach".'

'On Crete, you mean.'

She felt almost betrayed. 'Did you know that too?'

He nodded. 'I've looked at your stones many times while you've been asleep. But I shall never know how it is to feel them.'

'Then you're missing something important. Some of them are so smooth and round that they make me want to laugh.'

Ariel took off from the green wing chair and began rising towards the ceiling. As he floated about, he said, 'Now we've talked about all the five senses.'

'But there's a sixth sense too,' Cecilia interrupted.

'Is there?'

'Some people believe they have a sense that helps them to know things beyond their five ordinary senses. For instance, they can guess what will happen in the future. Or they know where something lost can be found. Other people think it's only superstition.'

He nodded as if sharing a secret. 'Perhaps that sense will help us to find the old Christmas star one day.'

'Do you *know* where it is?'

'We'll have to see . . .'

Cecilia lay thinking about Christmas. Then she said, 'I wonder whether the Christmas feeling has anything to do with the sixth sense. Perhaps we're a little more like the angels at Christmas time than we are during the rest of the year. And Christmas is about all the other senses. I can smell Christmas, I can taste Christmas, and I can see and hear it. And I can feel all the parcels and guess what's inside.'

There was a twinkle in Ariel's eye. 'Yes, what's inside. I'd like to talk about that too.'

'About what's inside the Christmas parcels?'

'No. About what's inside you.'

'Ugh, it sounds so disgusting.'

'That's peculiar.'

'What is?'

'That you humans think it's disgusting to talk about what you're made of. Imagine if a stone couldn't stand the thought of being a stone. It would be a very unhappy stone, for it would have to live with its own self-disgust for many thousands of years before it gradually dissolved into shingle and sand. But you don't last as long as that.'

'Then we'll have to talk about what's inside. But only on one condition.'

'And what is the condition?'

'That you promise to tell me lots of wonderful things about heaven afterwards.'

'Angels never break an agreement.'

'No. If they did, I'd lose faith in everything.'

'Perhaps *you* can tell me the answer to something we discuss in heaven all the time, and we often disagree strongly. It's a bit awkward to mention it, but . . .'

'Go on. Ask me!'

He took a deep breath. 'Can you feel your blood running in your veins?'

'Only when we bleed, or when we need to have a blood test. But that's when the blood runs out.'

'How does it feel?'

'Sometimes it just tickles, then it starts to smart afterwards.'

'But you must feel the flesh and blood which is inside you?'

She shook her head. 'I think we're made so that we don't feel what's beneath the skin. We can feel each other with our skin, but luckily we don't have to feel ourselves all the time.'

'You must feel *something*.'

She thought about it for a while, then shook her head. 'Nothing at all, as long as we're well. Only when something hurts.'

'Hurts?'

'When something pricks . . . or hits . . . or stings you.'

He threw up his arms in despair.

' "Pricks or hits or stings you".'

Cecilia said, 'Have you never tried pinching yourself in the arm?'

'No, never.'

'You ought to try, otherwise you can't be quite sure you're awake.'

Ariel tried to pinch himself in the arm, but Cecilia could see that he couldn't get hold of it properly. He shook his head.

'Angels can't pinch themselves in the arm,' he

admitted. 'We don't feel anything.'

'Then you can't know whether you're real.'

For a second – or even less than a second – it seemed as if Ariel had vanished. Perhaps she had just blinked.

When he was there again he said, 'We must hurry to get you back into bed.'

'Why?'

'It's seven o'clock. There are only a few seconds to go before the alarm clock rings. It's ringing now . . .'

CECILIA woke feeling heavy all over. Out of doors it was as light and clear as it can be at Christmas time.

She had only a vague memory of the night's adventures. Ariel had carried her down to the living room. Then he had carried her up again when the alarm clock rang in Mother's and Father's bedroom.

'Ariel!' she whispered.

But there was no answer. Perhaps he only came at night.

She rang the bell on the bedside table. It didn't take Mother much longer to come than it took Ariel to turn on the Christmas-tree lights. She was almost like a genie of the lamp too.

'So you're awake!' She knelt beside the bed. 'It's almost one o'clock. Have you been asleep all this time?'

She shook her head.

'What have you been doing, then?'

'I've been lying and looking and listening. There are sounds in a house at night too, if you use your ears properly. Sometimes I can hear it snowing outside.'

'And what have you been looking at?'

'There's such a lovely light coming through the window.'

'All you had to do was ring the bell.'

'I've been lying thinking about all sorts of things.'

'Have you been in pain?'

'No . . . now I am.'

'How does it feel?'

'Are you starting now?'

'What do you mean?'

'No, nothing. I feel awfully weak.'

'When I came in at seven o'clock you were sleeping like a log.'

'Logs don't sleep, Mother.'

'You were smiling in your sleep.'

'Logs can't smile either. Actually, I'd just fallen asleep when you came in.'

'Do you think so?'

'I heard the alarm ring.'

Mother put a hand on her forehead. 'Christine's come. She's downstairs in the living room, tasting Lars's marzipan sweets.'

'She's welcome to them.'

'What do you mean by that?'

'I don't want to hear about marzipan. Have you gone quite gaga?'

'No, I hope not.'

86

'Just send her up. I'm not afraid of injections any more.'

'We'd better take a trip to the bathroom first.'

'But Mother – '

'Yes?'

'Can't Christine just give me the injection, and have done with it?'

'I suppose so.'

'Often there's so much chat about how I'm feeling and what everything's called and all that. I'm tired of talking about it. Besides, it *is* Christmas Day.'

'She might want to look at you.'

'But you must be here. And if she starts sighing and groaning you must promise to chase her out. I don't know how to answer her anyway.'

'I'll try.'

'And Mother – I'm *going* to get well again. I promise.'

'Yes, of course you are.'

'But I'm the only one who's allowed to say that I'll get well soon. When *you* all say so, I think it's only to tease me.'

'You little monkey!'

Cecilia looked up. 'Are you crying?'

Mother wiped her eyes. 'No, of course not.'

'But you have tears in your eyes.'

'Oh, I've been peeling some onions.'

'*Again?*'

When Cecilia had been given her medicines and had

eaten a little, she was visited by each member of the family in turn. Lars had been out to test his mini-skis on the slopes down by the river. The whole of the river was frozen over; he couldn't even hear the water running under the ice. Some of the boys in the fifth and sixth classes had been skating where the river was at its widest point.

Father came up with a new number of *Science Illustrated*. Previously she had been given a whole pile of them. At the very beginning he had given her one with an article about minerals and gemstones: 'That's why the mountains are the treasure chests of the world.' She had read a few of the other articles as well; then she had asked for more. That had been a long time ago. Now Cecilia hadn't the strength to read very much at a time.

Grandad wanted to talk about the holiday trip to Crete. All of them had been there, Grandma and Grandad as well. At the same time they were told that Cecilia was ill. She couldn't quite remember whether it had been just before or just afterwards. She must have been to the first doctor, though.

It had been a 'dream holiday' – that was how the family described it. For two marvellous weeks they had been in the sun and on the beach and in exciting restaurants with funny waiters – while everyone else was at school or at work. One day they had visited the volcanic island, Santorini. They had sailed into the great crater left by the volcanic eruption three thousand five hundred years ago, when more than half of Santorini had sunk into the sea. To reach the town of Thera they had had to ride on mules up the steepest road Cecilia had ever seen. Then they had bathed on a lava beach where all the sand was black as coal and glowing hot because of the strong sun.

On some afternoons the whole family had walked along the big pebble beach and looked for beautiful stones. At the same time they had to keep an eye on the powerful surf which made the stones roll and rattle and run between their feet. Cecilia had been the judge. Only she was allowed to decide which stones were beautiful enough to justify taking up space in their luggage. They had brought several kilos home with them. Now Grandad wanted to be assured that *he* had found the best stone.

'We had a lovely time, Cecilia.'

Their dream holiday in Crete had been at the end of September. It was not since then that Cecilia had been completely well. But she had gone to school until the beginning of November. Then she had spent several weeks in hospital. After that her teacher had come a couple of times and told her what they were doing at school.

The last person to sit with her was Grandma. Ever since Cecilia was small she had told her stories. But she had never told her ordinary fairy tales. She told her about the old gods in whom the Vikings believed. Sometimes she read from Snorre's tales of the gods, and those stories were as good as any fairy tale. Recently she had read from a Children's Bible that Mother had when she was small. Imagine it being *so* old!

That day she told her about Odin's ravens. They were called Hugin and Munin and could fly all over the world to see how everything was. Hugin meant 'thought' and Munin meant 'mind'. In the evening the two ravens came back to Odin and told him what they had seen. So Odin learned how it was all over the world. But he was afraid, too, that one day they might not come back. Besides, the ravens were birds of carrion who helped Odin to find dead persons. Odin sat in the middle of Åsgard on a throne that was called Lidskjalv. Not only was he the wisest of all the gods, he was also the most melancholy, for Odin alone knew about Ragnarok – the great catastrophe to come.

Grandma told her a great deal about Odin and the two ravens. Later that afternoon Cecilia fell asleep. First she lay for a while, dozing, and then she slept properly. When she woke up she could hear the others eating dinner downstairs. They had just sat down, for Cecilia heard Mother say, 'I'll pass the soup round the table. We must make things easy.'

They always had cauliflower soup before the roast beef on Christmas Day.

Cecilia picked up the Chinese notebook from under her bed and started to turn the pages. A few weeks ago Grandma had given her a lovely pearl necklace, an old heirloom. Then she had written in the diary:

When I die a silver thread of smooth pearls will break, and the pearls will roll across the country and run home to their oyster mothers at the bottom of the sea. Who will dive for my pearls when I have gone? Who will know that they were mine? Who can guess that once the whole world was hanging round my neck?

She had begun chewing on her Biro while she thought over what she had talked about to the angel Ariel during the night. She tried to remember as much as she could, and then she wrote it down in the diary.

The angels in heaven can never be destroyed. That's because they do not have a body of flesh and blood that their soul can be parted from. That's not how it is in creation. Here everything is destroyed very easily. Even a mountain is slowly ground down and becomes earth and sand in the end. There's mischief afoot in nature. There's trouble brewing in creation.

You don't always understand completely what you have created. For instance, I can draw or paint something on a piece of paper. That doesn't mean I understand how it is to be the thing I've drawn. What I draw isn't alive, after all. And that's what is so strange: that I'm alive!

When she couldn't think of anything more to write, Cecilia put the book back on the floor and pushed it under the bed.

She must have slept again, for when she woke she heard a voice that said, 'Have you slept well?'

It was the angel Ariel. Cecilia looked up. He was kneeling at the foot of the bed.

'I've been here all the time,' he assured her.

'But I didn't see you.'

It took a little while for him to reply.

'Perhaps I didn't tell you that there are two kinds of angel visit. As a rule we simply sit with you without showing ourselves. On a very few occasions we reveal ourselves properly, as I'm doing now.'

'But both kinds are angel watches?'

'Yes, both kinds.'

'How was it when you sat with that boy in Germany who was ill?'

'I was simply there.'

'I don't really understand how you can be in the room when I can't see you.'

'It's not so difficult to explain.'

'Explain it, then!'

'If you dreamed that you were on a strange beach, wouldn't you say you had, in a way, been on that beach?'

'Ye-es, in a way.'

'But would the people who were on the beach have seen you?'

'No, of course not.'

'And you could travel there with a ticket from a travel agent and bathe on exactly the same beach. Then the people would see you, for then you would be revealing yourself properly.'

She looked up into the turquoise eyes. 'That was a clever comparison . . . By the way, you only just managed to get me into bed before Mother woke up.'

'Yes, by a hair's breadth.'

'If we hadn't managed it, she would have had a shock. Perhaps she would have thought that I was well again. "Oh, how nice, Cecilia. Imagine you're completely well again all of a sudden!"'

Ariel laughed. 'It's very strange to watch you sleeping.'

'I suppose angels never sleep?'

He shook his head. 'We don't understand what sleep is. Do you?'

'Not really.'

'But I'm sure you've thought about what happens inside your head just as you fall asleep.'

She shrugged her shoulders. 'I simply go out like a light.'

'I don't understand how you dare.'

'Why not?'

'You don't *know* whether you'll wake up again, after all . . . Can't you try to describe how it is to sleep?'

Cecilia sighed a little sigh.

'Just when we drop off, we're not awake, after all. I mean – we're in the borderland. That's why nobody knows exactly how it is to sleep.'

'Unbelievable, because a small revolution must take place inside your head.'

'But when that has happened, we're already asleep.

You see, you can't think, "Now I've fallen asleep." By then it's already too late to think. Your head is a bit like a machine that suddenly turns itself off.'

'But when it's turned itself off, and there's no more current in it, how does it manage to turn itself on again a few hours later?'

'You ask such difficult questions. We simply sleep, and then we wake up again a few hours later. Father has an alarm clock built inside his head. He wakes up at five to seven every single morning. Then he gets up and turns off the alarm clock that ought to have rung five minutes later.· But that's only on weekdays when he knows he has to get up. On Sundays he sleeps far longer. And then not even the alarm clock wakes him.'

The angel Ariel threw up his arms. 'I believe we're talking about the greatest mystery in the whole of heaven.'

'You've said that lots of times already.'

'But I'm not only thinking of things to do with sleep.'

'What *are* you thinking of, then?'

Cecilia pulled herself up in the bed, and Ariel looked her deep in the eyes.

'You humans are created of atoms and molecules on a small planet in space. You've been given skin and hair and five or six senses to enable you to experience the world around you. But inside that hard shell which is made of something similar to plaster or chalk, you also have a soft brain which gives you the ability to sleep and dream, think and remember.'

She glanced at the pearl necklace which was hanging round the Greek cat calendar.

'I told you I didn't like talking about what's inside my body,' she said.

'We must talk about your *soul*, Cecilia. Perhaps that's inside your body, too, but it's not a part of your body in exactly the same way as your heart and kidneys.'

She turned towards him again. 'Talk about the soul, then, and not about the heart and kidneys.'

'The most puzzling thing is what you call "memory". For instance, you can recognise a person you last saw long, long ago. If you were in a city and met the funny waiter again who tried to pull your hair all the time, you'd recognise him at once, even though he was in a market among hundreds of other people.'

'Were you on Crete too?'

He nodded. 'It doesn't make any difference to me whether you're in the living room or on Crete. You'd recognise him, wouldn't you?'

'I remember him very well.'

He had made himself comfortable.

'How does it feel inside your head when you "remember" something? What happens to all the atoms and molecules in your brain then? Do you think they suddenly jump back and take up exactly the same positions they were in when you experienced what you're thinking about?'

Cecilia gaped in astonishment. 'I've never thought about it like that before.'

He was a bit impatient now. 'Do you think the stones on a pebble beach will remember exactly how that beach looked only two minutes ago?'

'Oh no. Nothing is forgotten more quickly than the way stones are lying on a beach. In any case, stones can't remember anything at all.'

'But the atoms and molecules inside your head are able to "remember" how everything was many, many years ago – even though masses of new ideas and memories have washed up since then. Isn't a thought or a memory very like a certain pattern of pebbles on the beach of consciousness?'

She squirmed. '*You* remember as well. You said you could remember that Grandad had had pneumonia.'

'That's true, but I don't have a soul that's stitched together out of a few hundred thousand atoms and molecules.'

'What's *your* soul made of, then?'

'It has sprung straight out of God's mind.'

Cecilia thought for a while. Then she said, 'Perhaps my soul has too. Even though it consists of atoms and molecules, it may have sprung straight out of God's mind.'

He brushed this aside. 'However it is, we weren't supposed to be talking about heaven now.'

'You promised to talk about heaven.'

'Heaven can wait, Cecilia. Besides, when we talk about the human soul, we're talking about something very close to heaven.'

She looked up at the ceiling. 'Grandma says the soul is divine.'

'She's obviously a very wise grandmother.'

'And she knows the Bible and Snorre's sagas almost by heart.'

'Exactly! There it comes again!'

'What does?'

'Just *how* she knows something "by heart" is part of the great puzzle we're talking about. Has it occurred to you that the human brain is the most puzzling substance in the whole of space?'

'Not until now.'

'All the atoms that your brain is made of were once distilled on a star. But then they were meshed together in an extraordinary way and became something that you humans call "consciousness". The human soul flickers past in a brain that is woven together of some particles of dust which, once upon a time, drifted down from the stars in the sky. Human thoughts and feelings play over and over again on this fine star dust in which all the nerve wires can be connected in eternally new ways.'

'Then maybe there's some dust from the Star of Bethlehem in my brain.'

'And in the thoughts you think, in all the memories you have.'

She tried to look out of the window while he went on talking.

'It must feel queer to be a living brain in space. It's like a separate little universe inside the big universe outside. Because there are just as many atoms and molecules in your brain as there are stars and planets in space.'

She interrupted him.

'And maybe it's just as far in to my innermost thoughts as it is to the furthest stars in space.'

He nodded. 'The difference is that only a brain is conscious of itself. It can judge its own actions all the time. The firmament outside it can't do that. Space can't, as it were, lift itself up and say, "I am I". Space needs human help to do that.'

She smiled triumphantly. 'I agree that that's an important difference.'

'But you haven't explained yet how it *feels* to remember anything.'

'I'd forgotten that.'

'*That*'s quite interesting too.'

'What is?'

' "I'd forgotten that." Perhaps you can explain instead how it is to forget something?'

'It just disappears.'

' "It just disappears"!' repeated Ariel. This time he tried to mimic her voice too.

'But then it may suddenly pop up again. Sometimes I have it on the tip of my tongue.'

'On the tip of your tongue?'

'That's what we say.'

'I didn't think that had anything at all to do with memory. You're not going to tell me that humans taste words in exactly the same way as you taste a strawberry?'

Cecilia laughed. ' "I think I know," I say. As long as nobody disturbs me, it usually pops up again. Grandad says we must never worry about a thought that escapes us.'

'Why not?'

'It's like a fish suddenly slipping off the hook. It simply swims down deep again and comes back even fatter.'

Ariel nodded emphatically. 'Then maybe they're right.'

'Who are?'

'There are some angels who like saying that we'll never get to understand earthly matters. But I've never wanted to give up. I've always tried to understand completely how it is to be a human of flesh and blood.'

'I'm not so sure I can help you, for I don't understand it myself.'

Ariel had begun to rise from the foot of the bed. As he hovered around the room he said, 'Can you re-member the first thing I said when we met?'

She had to think. 'I know you were sitting on the windowsill. But I don't think I remember exactly what you said.'

' "Don't think I remember . . ." '

'Didn't you just say "Hi" or something like that?'

He shook his head, and a long time passed. Finally

Cecilia began waving her arm. 'Wait a bit! It's on the tip of my tongue.'

'Then I think you should spit it out before it suddenly "disappears" again.'

He sat on the windowsill just as he had done when he appeared the first time. Cecilia looked up at him and said, 'You asked whether I had slept well.'

'Congratulations!'

'That wasn't so difficult.'

'But I was witness to a great mystery. I asked whether you remembered something, and you answered that you had forgotten it. Quite gone! But when you didn't remember it, exactly how was it then?'

Cecilia sighed in despair. 'I agree it's odd to think about. Sometimes something suddenly occurs to me.'

'And from exactly where does it occur to you?'

'From my head.'

Ariel took his time. 'And exactly where does it occur to you?'

She had to laugh. 'In my head!'

'So, *from* your head *to* your head. And yet we're talking about one and the same head all the time. But it's not only what humans see and hear that is remembered and forgotten – and then remembered again. The brain acts on its own as well. That's what you call "thinking". That's as if all the pebbles on the big beach began to move without any help from the waves.'

Cecilia laughed again. 'I'm trying to imagine it. What if they just began jumping all over the place!'

'And a thought you've thought – for instance, that a Christmas tree star has disappeared – can be pushed aside for a while, but can then be brought back into your consciousness again. It's as if you wind your consciousness back in order to think exactly the same thought over again. I believe you rewind many reruns of old thoughts which in fact ought to have been completely thought out long ago.'

'I'd rather say that a thought pops up again by itself. We can't always decide what we're going to remember and what we're going to forget. Sometimes we think about things we don't want to think about. At other times we make a slip of the tongue. Then we say things we hadn't really thought of saying. Occasionally it can be very embarrassing!'

The angel Ariel remained sitting on the windowsill, nodding and nodding his shining head. 'Then it is perhaps as I feared,' he said.

'What?'

'You don't have only one soul like us. In a way you have two – or many more, for that matter. How would you otherwise explain that you think about things you don't *want* to think about?'

'I don't know.'

'Such unwanted thoughts must be guided by something other than your own consciousness. It must be a bit like a theatre where you haven't any idea what play will be put on next time.'

'Do you mean that the soul is the theatre, and that all

the actors on the stage are the different thoughts that keep on appearing and playing different roles?'

'A bit like that. There must, in any case, be many rooms in the theatre of consciousness. There must be many different stages as well.'

He took off from the windowsill, hovered in a great arc above the floor and sat down again at the foot of Cecilia's bed.

'Can you try to describe how it feels inside your head when you think of something?' he said.

'I don't feel anything.'

'Isn't it true that it tickles when you think funny thoughts? Doesn't it smart a bit too if you think about something that's unpleasant and sad?'

'In a way it tickles when I think about something that's fun. Perhaps it smarts to think about something sad too. But it doesn't tickle or smart inside my head. It's in my soul, and my soul isn't exactly the same as my head.'

'I would have thought the nerve wires would itch a little,' he objected.

Cecilia looked challengingly at the angel Ariel.

'You're not going to tell me that angels don't think, either?'

'Yes, I have to say that, for angels are not allowed to tell lies.'

'Now I think you're going too far!'

'But we don't think in the same way as humans of flesh and blood. We don't need to "think things over" in order to find an answer to something. All that we know, and all that we *can* know, is at the front of our consciousness all at once. God has allowed us to understand a tiny fraction of his great mystery, but not everything. So we ought to keep silent about what we do not understand.'

Cecilia thought through it all.

'Then it's different for us. We try all the time to understand more and more. Suddenly a new idea dawns on us. The cleverest people get the Nobel Prize for their discoveries, if they're very important to everybody. It's a bit like when the body grows. Our understanding grows too.'

'But then you can forget things. So you take two steps forward and one back.'

'Maybe. But even if we do forget something, it doesn't have to disappear completely. It can pop up again all of a sudden like a jack-in-the-box.'

'That's the big difference between humans and angels. We don't know what it means to forget something, so we don't know what it feels like to remember anything either. I know neither more nor less today than I did two thousand years ago. Not all the angels are happy about this difference.'

'I didn't know you could be envious.'

He laughed. 'It doesn't go as deep as that.'

'Can your thoughts go deep, then? Grandad says now and again that he has thought some very deep thoughts.'

He shook his head. 'Because all our thoughts are at the front of our consciousness at the same time, we never experience the joy of surprising ourselves with sudden profound ideas. We don't have that kind of borderland to draw on. Our consciousness doesn't move on a stormy sea where ideas we have once forgotten can suddenly reappear like fat fish from the depths.'

'You said angels didn't sleep.'

'No, we never sleep, so we don't dream either. What does that feel like?'

'I don't *feel* anything.'

He gave a brief nod. 'Just as I can't feel myself hovering in the air, just as I don't feel myself picking up a snowball.'

'Dreaming is a way of thinking,' she said. 'Or a way of seeing. Or maybe both at once. But when we dream, we don't decide for ourselves what we're thinking or seeing.'

'You must explain that.'

'When we dream, our heads think all by themselves. That's when you can begin to talk about a real theatre. Sometimes I wake up and remember that I've dreamt a whole play, or a whole film.'

'Which you create yourself, because you play all the characters.'

'Yes, in a way.'

He became enthusiastic. 'Perhaps we can say that the brain cells show each other films. At the same time the film sits right at the back of the cinema and watches itself on the screen.'

'That's an odd thing to say! "The brain cells show each other films." I think I can imagine that.'

'Because when you humans dream, you are film stars and audience at one and the same time. Isn't that mysterious?'

She retreated. 'I think this is an eerie subject to talk about.'

'But it must be fun to experience it. You witness a whole firework display of thoughts and pictures inside your own head, even though you haven't helped to fire a single rocket. It must almost be like a free show.'

She nodded. 'It can be great fun, but it can be frightening too, because we don't always dream nice dreams. We can dream ugly, horrible dreams as well.'

He was very understanding now. 'Of course it's a shame if you worry yourselves like that. Ideally you ought to have had the possibility of shutting out a dream if you didn't enjoy it. There ought to be an emergency exit in the cinema. But because the cinema is your own soul, which in addition decides on the whole pro-gramme, that's quite impossible. Because you can't run away from your own souls. You can't bite your own tails. Or perhaps that's exactly what you *do* do: you bite your own tails until you shout and scream in fear and terror.'

Cecilia had begun biting her nails. 'I don't want it to

be like that,' she said. 'But I can't simply decide for myself to dream pleasant dreams. I have to put up with what comes. After a long night I can wake up and believe I've been on Crete; and in a way I *have* been there, because in my dream I believe I'm where the dream is taking place.'

Ariel studied her with his clear, determined, sapphire gaze. 'Just so!'

'What?'

'Wait a bit! Can you dream that you can fly too, or that you can pass through locked doors?'

'Yes, of course. Anything can happen in a dream, at least, almost anything. I don't even need to fall asleep. I can let my thoughts roam when I'm wide awake. I can fly around the house here, or go to foreign countries. Once I dreamed I was on the moon. Marianne and I had found a spacecraft behind the old dairy. So we simply pressed a button and off we went.'

Ariel had begun hovering aloft near the ceiling again. After a little trip round the room he alighted on the chair beside the bed.

'Then it's in the can,' he said.

Cecilia shook her head helplessly. 'I don't understand you at all.'

He pointed at her forehead and said, 'In your thoughts humans can do everything angels can do with their bodies. When you dream, you can do exactly the same inside your heads as the angels can do all over creation.'

She felt slightly confused. 'I've never thought about it.'

'But there's more,' continued Ariel. 'When you humans dream, nothing can harm you. You're just as safe as the angels in heaven. Everything you experience is purely and simply consciousness, and you don't make use of the body's five senses.'

Cecilia was struck by a completely new idea. She sat up straight and said, in a firm voice, 'In that case maybe our souls are immortal! Maybe they're just as immortal as the angels' in heaven!'

He hesitated.

'Now you understand a little better, at any rate, how it is to be an angel. Even though we've mostly talked about how it is to be a human, made of flesh and blood, you understand a little more about heavenly matters as well. Because heaven is reflected on earth.'

She tried again. 'And the soul is divine, isn't that so?'

When he didn't answer, it occurred to her that she had to try to keep him from disappearing.

'You promised to tell me more,' she said.

He nodded. 'But right now your mother is on her way up from the living room, so I must hurry through the looking-glass.'

She looked round the room. 'Which looking-glass are you always talking about?'

He had left the chair and was walking across the floor.

As he did so his outline faded more and more. As he vanished, he said, 'The whole of creation is a looking-glass, Cecilia. The whole world is a mystery.'

MANY days passed without the angel Ariel appearing again, but one of the family was always sitting on the chair beside the bed. Christine came to visit almost every day, even though Mother and Grandma had learned how to give the injections. Cecilia didn't always know which day it was, or what time of day. When she could manage it, she wrote down a few new thoughts in the Chinese notebook.

The skis and the toboggan were leaning up against the wall between her and her parents' bedroom. It was still winter, with good snow for skiing. Cecilia was determined to get better before the snow thawed. She couldn't bear to wait a whole year to get out on the ski tracks again.

She never mentioned Ariel to any of the others. He had nothing to do with the rest of the family, for even though Cecilia was a member of the family at Skotbu, she was also a person standing quite alone between heaven and earth.

But what had become of him? Hadn't he promised to tell her more about heavenly matters? Hadn't he said, too, that angels never tell lies?

Surely he hadn't deceived her? Had he got Cecilia to tell him a whole lot about how it is to be a human made of flesh and blood, and then just made off again without keeping his side of the bargain?

She opened her eyes. At almost the same moment Mother appeared in the doorway and came to sit on the edge of the bed. Cecilia stared up at her with an empty expression.

'Have you been slicing onions again?' she mumbled.

She shook her head. All the same, Cecilia said, 'You eat far too many onions.'

Mother stroked her hair.

'It's nearly midnight. The others went to bed long ago. Now I'm going to try to sleep for a bit too.'

'*Try* to sleep?'

'No, no . . . I'll take a pill.'

'You mustn't make a habit of it.'

'There's no danger of that.'

Cecilia looked up. 'I wonder why we're made so that we have to sleep.'

'It's a way of resting. Some people think we need to dream as well.'

'Why?'

Mother took a deep breath – and breathed out again. 'I don't know.'

'But I think *I* know the answer.'

'Do you?'

'I think we need to dream because we need to dream ourselves far away.'

'You think a lot of strange things, Cecilia.'

'Lots of people suffer so much that perhaps they would have died of sorrow if they couldn't dream something nice in between all the sadnesses.'

Mother washed Cecilia's face with a damp cloth and changed her nightdress.

'You mustn't mind me being so weak. I think I *am* a little better.'

'Maybe . . .'

'Didn't Christine say so too?'

She hesitated. 'She said we must wait and see.'

'Perhaps I can get up for a while tomorrow. At coffee-time, maybe.'

'We must take one day at a time.'

'But soon I'm going to try on my new skis. You promised.'

'They're there, ready for you. Now be sure you ring the bell, even if you only want to talk to someone. Father will come soon to sit with you.'

'There's no need.'

'But we want to.'

'You mustn't be surprised if you hear me talking to myself, will you?'

'Do you usually do that?'

Cecilia looked up at her again. 'I don't know.'

Mother put her arms round her and gave her a hug.

'You're the best girl in the whole world,' she said. 'Without you the world would be miserable and empty.'

Cecilia smiled. 'That was a solemn good-night wish.'

She slept almost as soon as Mother was out of the room. After a while she was woken by someone tapping on the window pane. She opened her eyes and saw Ariel's face outside. In the golden light from the tree in the garden he reminded her of a picture she had seen once in *Science Illustrated* of a golden angel from Russia. Or had it been the Christchild?

He waved, and the next moment dived straight through the window and stood in front of the desk. The window pane was as whole as before.

Cecilia opened her eyes wide. 'Even though we've talked a lot, I don't understand how you manage to do that.'

Ariel came towards her and sat on the wooden chair. It was as well Father hadn't come in yet.

'It's not so important either,' he said. 'That's why there's no point in talking about it.'

Cecilia sat up in bed, with one leg on top of the duvet.

'Where *have* you been?' she asked.

'You've had so many other visitors,' he replied.

Cecilia nodded. 'Is that the only reason you haven't been here for such a long time?'

He didn't answer her question.

'The moon's almost full,' he boasted. 'It's as light as

a quarter of daylight outside when the moonlight floods over the snow-covered landscape.'

'Wonderful! I'd have loved to come out with you to see the moon with my own eyes.'

'Can't you do that?'

'I *am* much better.'

'That's super! It got a bit boring when you were so poorly all the time.'

'Would I be allowed?'

The angel Ariel took off from the wooden chair and began to hover around the toboggan and the skis.

'Of course your mother and father wouldn't allow you to go out in the middle of the night.'

'But will *you* allow me to?'

He nodded confidentially. Cecilia had kicked off the duvet already.

'When you're allowed to do something by the angels in heaven, it doesn't matter what the others say,' she said. 'Besides, the whole house is asleep.'

'A short way, then. But you must dress well so that you don't turn into one big peppermint lump.'

Cecilia stood up and walked across the floor. She stood quite steady. She didn't feel the least bit dizzy.

'I'm going to try out the skis,' she said.

The next moment she was standing in front of the clothes cupboard. As far back as the beginning of November she had made sure all her winter clothes were ready, so they were lying on a separate shelf. She took off her nightdress and found her vest, long johns, sweater, ski trousers and anorak. She found a scarf and a woolly hat, ski mitts and thick socks. Soon she was sitting on the edge of the bed, lacing up her ski boots. When she was ready, she glanced up at Ariel.

'Can you be bothered to carry my skis for me?'

They went out into the corridor and crept downstairs to the ground floor. Cecilia unlocked the front door and let Ariel out with the skis. Then she followed, closing the door carefully behind her.

They went past the barn. Here a steep slope ran down to the stream and the big fir wood. Cecilia placed her ski boots in the bindings and slipped the loops of her ski poles round her wrists. The moonlight threw sharp shadows on to the snow.

'I'll try to ski down the slope,' she said. 'You'll have to run after me, because I've waited so long to do this.'

And she set off downhill. But the angel Ariel didn't run behind her; he began hovering in the air close by her side.

'Now we're both flying,' he said. 'The only difference is that I don't feel anything.'

'It's marvellous!' shouted Cecilia. 'Quite angelically marvellous!'

When they were down on the level, Cecilia fell in the loose snow and this made both of them laugh.

She picked herself up and pointed at the fir wood.

'There's a good track that goes up to Ravens' Hill.

From there you have a view over the whole valley.'

For a moment he seemed to be summing her up, but it was only a brief moment.

'Can you manage to go all the way?'

She had already set off. 'Just now I feel as strong as an ox!' she shouted.

She poled her way into a deep ski track, and Ariel darted round her like a flying dog on a Sunday outing, now on her right, now on her left. Every so often he ran on his feet too.

'Don't you feel cold, walking in the snow with bare feet?' she asked.

He sighed indulgently. 'Surely we're not going to begin at the beginning again?'

Cecilia laughed. 'It's just that it seems so crazy. Did you know there are fakirs who can turn off all their senses, so that they neither freeze nor burn themselves? They can even sleep on a bed of nails.'

He nodded. 'We're in India just as often as in Norway.'

They entered the wood where the track curved between the closely planted tree trunks. Sometimes Ariel took a short cut and glided right through them. Once he shot through a solid thicket. The thicket was a mere wisp of fog to him.

Cecilia had to herringbone up the last slope of Ravens' Hill in order to keep her skis from slipping. Soon they were standing right at the top of the little crest where there were no trees. Cecilia lifted one of her ski poles and pointed across the frozen landscape that lay bathed in blue moonlight.

'When I was small I thought this was the roof of the world,' she said. 'And when Grandma told me about Odin who sat on his throne and looked out over the world, I imagined that he was sitting here. You've heard about his two ravens, haven't you?'

Ariel nodded. 'Hugin and Munin. That means "thought" and "mind".'

'Grandma said that too. Because in a way they were his own thoughts and his own mind that he was sending round the world.'

Ariel nodded again. Then he said something strange.

'Perhaps you remember that we talked about "the inner eye" which all humans have, but which is of most importance to people who are blind. That, too, consists of "thought" and "mind". Hugin and Munin were Odin's inner eye.'

Cecilia stared open-mouthed. Why hadn't she thought of that before?

The angel Ariel went on: 'God is omniscient and he can be in several places at once. Odin couldn't do that, but at least he had the two ravens. That's how he became a little omniscient too.'

Cecilia lifted her ski pole and pointed out over the valley again.

'Do you see all the farms?' she asked. 'I know somebody in nearly every house. That's the school down there . . . that white stripe curving through the landscape is the river. It's called the Leira. Marianne lives in the yellow house on the other side.'

'I know that, Cecilia.'

'Down there on the left we can just see the lights of Kløfta, and the peak far beyond is called Witches' Hill. Jessheim is in the other direction.'

Ariel nodded. 'I know all about it.'

'Down there you can see our barn. You can see a bit of the house, too, behind the big tree with the lights. The window to the left on the first floor is my room.'

'I've gone in through that window many times,' said Ariel.

He started to hover a foot above the ground so that he could look into Cecilia's eyes while they talked. His blue-green sapphire eyes glittered in the light from the moon.

'If you had been standing in your window down there,' he said, 'and looked up at Ravens' Hill now, you would have been able to see us up here on the summit. Then we might have waved to you.'

Cecilia put a hand to her mouth. Wasn't that rather a strange thing to say? She knew that something about it wasn't exactly right, but she couldn't quite grasp what it was.

'Father may come into my room at any moment,' she said, 'to see if I'm asleep. If he comes now, he'll get a shock. "Goodness me!" he'd say. "The bird has flown the nest!"'

'Would you like me to see if he's asleep?'

'*Can* you do that?'

For a short while Ariel was gone, and Cecilia was left standing all alone between heaven and earth. For a few seconds it felt as if she had lost a twin brother. Then he was standing right beside her again.

'Both of them are asleep,' he assured her. 'She's lying with her head under his chin. They've set the alarm for half past three.'

Cecilia sighed with relief. She pointed at the landscape again.

'I've never understood how the moon manages to throw out so much light.'

'It's because everything else is completely dark. When the light shines in the darkness, not so much as a single ray is lost.'

'But the moon doesn't really give light by itself,' protested Cecilia. 'It's only a mirror that borrows its light from the sun.'

Ariel nodded solemnly. 'The sun doesn't really give light by itself either. It's only a mirror that borrows its light from God.'

'Is that true?'

'I don't stand here in the sight of God in order to deceive you.'

'No, of course not. It's just that I've never thought of the sun borrowing light from God in the same way as the moon borrows light from the sun.'

She leaned on her ski poles and stared down into the snow. When she looked up again, Ariel had moved.

Now he was hovering a few inches above the ground right in front of her.

He said, 'You borrow your light from God too, Cecilia. You are God's mirror too. For what would you be without the sun, and what would the sun be without God?'

Cecilia smiled broadly. 'That makes me a little moon as well.'

'And right now you're shining on me.'

'You say such odd things. Everything becomes so solemn that it sends shivers down my spine.'

The angel Ariel nodded. 'When we talk about the glory of heaven it does get a little solemn.'

'Are you going to tell me about heaven now?'

'I've started already.'

He pointed up at the vault of heaven. The moon was shining so strongly that only a few stars were showing themselves as pale dots in the night.

'First of all you must understand that you're in heaven already,' he said.

'Is *this* heaven?'

The angel Ariel nodded. 'Where else should we be? The earth is only a tiny speck in the enormous firmament.'

'I've never thought about it quite like that.'

'This is Heavenly Earth, Cecilia. This is the Garden of Eden where humans live. The angels live in all the other places as well.'

'Do you mean in space?'

'Or in the firmament, but it's exactly the same.'

Cecilia leaned over her ski poles again and stared down into the snow. 'It's mysterious,' she said. 'Very mysterious.'

When she looked up again, Ariel gave her a challenging look. '*I* think it's very easy to understand.'

Cecilia shook her head in frustration.

'I've always wondered where heaven *is*,' she said. 'None of the astronauts have caught sight of either God or the angels.'

'No brain surgeon has caught sight of a thought in the brain either. And no scholar has ever seen another person's dream. That doesn't mean that thoughts and dreams don't exist inside people's heads.'

'Of course not.'

'And nobody on the big beach could see you when you dreamed yourself back there. We've talked about this plenty of times already.'

'Do you mean that there are swarms of angels out in the universe?'

'Indeed there are. You surely don't think God created such a big universe without having any reason for it? Since we can't freeze or burn ourselves, we can exist on absolutely all the celestial bodies. Only here on earth is it suitably cold and suitably warm for humans of flesh and blood. Everywhere else it would be either much too hot or much too cold. If the earth were only a fraction closer to the sun, it would have been quite unbearable for human flesh and blood. And if the earth were only a fraction closer to Pluto, you would have immediately frozen into ice sculptures.'

The angel took a little turn in the air, but he soon returned to a mere couple of feet above the ground in front of Cecilia.

'Have you been on the moon?' she asked.

He answered at once, 'That's where I ballet-dance.'

'On the moon?'

He nodded. 'It was quite a joke when the first humans arrived. There was a whole crowd of us there, you see. But neither Armstrong nor the other astronauts could see us. They thought they were all alone. And they were so proud because they thought they were the first to visit the moon. Do you know what Armstrong said when he went out of the moon-landing craft?'

'"One small step for a man, one giant leap for mankind",' answered Cecilia.

'Exactly!'

Cecilia felt a little cross on behalf of mankind because the angels had spied on the first astronauts, who had thought they were alone on the moon.

'I'd like to write about that in the paper,' she said. '"Latest news: there are swarms of angels on the moon. New radar reveals old secret."'

Ariel laughed. 'But perhaps you haven't heard of the asteroids?'

Cecilia was delighted, for now she was on her home ground. She had read more about space than most children of her age. When she was first ill, she had ploughed through the large pile of *Science Illustrated*.

'Of course,' she answered. 'They're those tiny planets that orbit the sun. But there are so many of them and they're so small that they haven't been given any proper names. Many of them have only a number.'

Ariel clapped his hands. 'Bravo! So you know more about the glory of heaven than you thought. If I want to be completely alone – for fifty or a hundred years, for instance – I usually sit on a small asteroid. Because even though there are plenty of angels in heaven, there are even more asteroids. Pottering about on a tiny planet can be very soothing after an upsetting angel discussion at a large meeting. Sometimes I play hopscotch from asteroid to asteroid. That's terrific fun!'

Cecilia thought it all sounded much too simple. 'I think you're telling lies,' she said.

She looked up into the blue-green sapphire eyes, but dropped her gaze quickly when she saw that she had made such a serious accusation.

'Pity,' said Ariel. 'Because no angel tells lies, so you can't believe I'm an angel either.'

'Tell me more, then,' replied Cecilia sullenly.

'The thing I find most fun of all is sitting on a comet,' he said.

'On a comet?'

'Yes. Halley's comet, for example. It takes seventy-six years to orbit the sun. But its track is slung so far out into space that it travels terribly fast. Sitting on a comet can perhaps be compared with riding on a roller-coaster. The only difference is that you don't have to climb up again to slide down.'

Cecilia shook her head. 'I wouldn't object to that,' she said. 'I'd love to have done that myself. But I didn't know angels were so playful.'

The angel Ariel looked into her eyes.

'I told you God created Adam and Eve so that there should be someone to run among all the trees and play hide-and-seek in the big garden. Because there was no point in creating a big garden if there were no children to play in it.'

Cecilia nodded, and Ariel continued: 'There's no point either in having enormous space, with billions of stars and planets, moons and asteroids, if there are no angels to enjoy all that splendour.'

Cecilia hesitated. 'I agree that it sounds fairly reasonable. But not so much as a hint of what you're saying is to be found in any Bible story.'

Ariel didn't reply to that. He said something quite different.

'If God had created everything simply to show his power he would have been fearfully self-centred. There are about one hundred billion galaxies in the universe, and in each one of all those galaxies there are about one hundred billion suns. So you can only guess how many planets and moons there are, quite apart from all the asteroids. Even though there are many angels as well, we can't exactly complain that we've been given too little space to play in. We can't complain about having too little time either.'

'No, I'm sure you can't. You're welcome to it.'

'We are the ones who bind the universe together, Cecilia. God has never had any ravens on his shoulders, but he has always had a whole host of angels.'

Cecilia had begun digging in the snow with one of her ski poles.

She said, 'If you had written a book about these things you'd probably have been given a Nobel Prize or two.'

'Why two?'

'One in theology and one in astronomy. Unless they were to combine them, of course. At the worst you could risk getting a Nobel Prize in imagination. It would have been well deserved.'

Ariel laughed.

'Well, I'm not going to enter into competition with serious scholars like that. They believe that all the secrets of nature can be revealed with microscopes and telescopes. And then they believe only in what can be weighed and measured. But they understand only in part. They don't understand that they see everything in a glass, darkly. It's impossible to weigh or measure an angel. Nor does it help to examine a mirror in a microscope. The result is that you merely see your own reflection even more clearly. So it's better to use a little imagination.'

Cecilia dug more and more energetically in the snow.

'I'd like,' she said, 'to play hopscotch among the

asteroids. I'd like to ballet-dance on the moon or to cling tight to a fun comet that floated around in space. Because all of it's in heaven, you said . . .'

'Yes?'

'Many people believe we go to heaven when we die. Do we?'

Ariel sighed heavily. 'You *are* all in heaven now. Right now you're here. So I think you should all stop quarrelling and fighting. Actually it's not very good manners to fight in the sight of God.'

'You didn't answer my question.'

'You come and go, go your ways and come back. The stars and the planets do so too.'

'Blah, blah!'

Cecilia struck the ground with her ski pole.

'You shouldn't be angry, Cecilia.'

She knew the angel was right, but she thought she should be allowed to be a little angry at the moment.

She said, 'You've gone on and on talking about humans being made of flesh and blood. But nothing that is made of flesh and blood has eternal life, you said. I think that's a great pity, because in fact I, too, could consider playing hopscotch among all the asteroids for a few thousand years before taking a couple of million years' holiday on an exotic planet in a distant galaxy. That's why I'm terribly curious to know whether we have eternal life.'

She put her hand to her mouth. Where had all those words come from?

Ariel said, 'Nobody has "eternal life", not the angels in heaven, at any rate. Because angels don't "live", which is why we can't feel anything, and why we don't grow up to be adults either. We've talked about this already.'

Cecilia looked down at the snow.

'I think it's a bit much to complain that you're not alive when you can fly around among stars and planets for ever.'

'Just as you fly around on distant beaches when you sleep,' replied Ariel. 'What if your whole life had been only a dream!'

Cecilia shrugged her shoulders.

'If only that dream had lasted for ever, and had been good fun as well, I think I'd have preferred the dream. What would *you* have preferred, anyway: a human life for a few years or an angel life for ever and ever?'

'Neither you nor I have had such a choice, so it's not worth talking about. Besides, it must be better to look out over the firmament one single time than not to experience anything at all. Those who are not yet created have no claim to be created either.'

Cecilia thought over the last part of what Ariel had said. Then she thought it over once more. Finally she said, 'But maybe they'd prefer not to be created than to live for only a short while. If they hadn't been created, they wouldn't know what they were missing, you see.'

Ariel didn't reply. Suddenly he shot upwards and peered down at the house.

'It's three o'clock,' he said. 'We must hurry before they wake up.'

Cecilia skied downhill all the way. The angel Ariel fluttered beside her. It didn't matter that the track between the trees was narrow, because Cecilia managed to stay upright on it, and Ariel simply passed through the tree trunks as if they were marking sticks. Before long they were tramping up the last rise towards the barn.

Ariel caught Cecilia by her anorak hood and said, 'There's no time to go round.'

'No time?'

But Ariel had no time to reply either. He seized her anorak and lifted her high in the air. The next moment they dived in through the closed window and were standing in the middle of Cecilia's room.

The window pane was whole as before, and so was Cecilia. But she still had her skis on. Water had begun dripping all over the floor.

'What *do* you think they'll say?' she whispered, pointing guiltily at the skis and the floor.

'I'll fix it,' said the angel Ariel.

Cecilia took off her skis and her clothes like lightning, pulled on her nightdress, and crept into bed. She watched how the angel folded her clothes neatly in double-quick time and laid them back in the cupboard. He leant the skis and poles up against the wall. Then he blew on the skis and the floor a few times, and all the water and slush disappeared. It was impossible to tell that Cecilia had been on an outing in the moonlight.

'Super!' said Cecilia, and fell asleep.

WHEN she opened her eyes, Father was sitting on the chair beside the bed.

'What's the time?' she asked.

'Seven o'clock.'

'Have you been here long?'

'Only a few hours . . .'

Then she remembered her ski trip in the middle of the night. She peered across the room. Nobody could have seen that she had used the skis.

Maybe it hadn't been last night. Maybe several days had passed, for all Cecilia knew.

She felt weaker than ever. Could that be because of the ski trip with Ariel?

'I don't feel very well,' she said.

He took her hand. 'No, you're not very well either.'

'What day is it?'

He looked at his watch. 'January the twenty-second.'

'Almost a month since Christmas Eve.'

He nodded. 'Mother will be here soon with your injection.'

'With my injection?'

'Yes. She's in the bathroom.'

'I'm fed up with the whole lousy business.'

He squeezed her hand. 'Of course you are,' was all he said.

She tried to look up at him. 'When I'm grown up I'm going to study astronomy.'

'That's . . . tremendously exciting.'

'*Someone*'s got to find out all about it in the end.'

'What are you thinking about now?'

'I'm the one who's ill, Father . . .'

'Yes, that's·true.'

' . . . but you're the ones who aren't paying attention. I mean, someone ought to find out how everything *is*. It can't just go on like this.'

'Science finds out a little more all the time.'

'Do you believe in angels?'

'Why do you wonder about that?'

'Do you believe in God, then?'

He nodded. 'You believe in him too, don't you?'

'I don't know . . . if only he weren't so silly. Did you know that he's put an angel on almost every single asteroid? If they want to, they can sit there and enjoy themselves for ever and ever. They don't even need to cut their nails or clean their teeth. Other angels sit on enormous comets that travel round the sun at terrific speed. Then they look down at the earth and are *very* inquisitive about how it feels to be a human being made of flesh and blood . . .'

'Now I think you're imagining things.'

' . . . while Almighty God sits back comfortably and blows bubbles with us. Just to show off to the angels in heaven.'

'I'm sure he doesn't do that.'

'How can you be so sure? Supposing he's just a rotten swindler?'

'We don't understand everything, Cecilia.'

'I've heard that before. We understand only in part. We see everything in a glass, darkly . . . '

'Yes, those are wise words.'

Cecilia looked up at him with a resigned expression.

There was a long silence. She wanted to say some more, but she didn't know whether she had the strength. It was as if she hoped Father would pull the words out of her head without her having to open her mouth.

She said, 'Do you remember when we went to Crete?'

He tried to smile. 'How should I manage to forget it?'

'I mean do you remember the plane journey, dumb-bell?'

He nodded. 'I even remember that we had chicken with potato salad on the way there, and meatballs in paprika sauce on the way home.'

'Don't talk about food, Father. I mean that I looked out of the window. I looked down on the earth.'

She said no more. But she thought about how she had

sat high up in the sky and looked down on the earth with all its cities and roads, mountains and fields. On the way home they had flown above the clouds at first. It had been as if she found herself midway between heaven and earth. They had not come home to Norway until late at night. When they flew in to the airfield they had dived down beneath all that Christmas cotton wool. And there was revealed a magical country with electric lights in all the colours of the rainbow.

She said, 'When we come into the world, we are given the whole world as a gift.'

Father nodded. He looked as if he didn't like her having so much to talk about.

'But it's not only ourselves who come to the world. You might just as well say that it's the world that comes to us.'

'It's almost the same.'

'I feel as if I own the whole world, Father.'

He took her other hand. 'In a way you do.'

'Not just this house . . . and Ravens' Hill . . . and the river down there. I own a bit of the Lasithi plain in Crete . . . and the whole of the island of Santorini. It's just as if I had lived once upon a time in the old castle at Knossos. The sun and the moon and all the stars in the sky are mine. Because I've *seen* them all.'

Father took the bell from the bedside table and rang it. Why did he do that? Surely he didn't feel ill, too?

She continued. 'Nobody can take any of it away from

me. It will always be *my* world. This will be my world for ever and ever.'

Then Mother came in and Father got up and rushed out. He had been sitting with her for so long that he was probably desperate to go to the loo.

'Cecilia?'

She turned towards her mother with an accusing look.

'Cecilia!'

'Can't you just give me the injection, Mother? We don't need to talk about anything.'

She was given the injection at once, and then she must have slept again, because the next time she woke Ariel was sitting on the chair beside the bed.

She felt much better than she had when Mother and Father had been there. Maybe she was revived by being with the angel?

'Have you slept well?' he asked.

She pulled herself up and sat on the edge of the bed, looked over at the window and saw that it was light outside.

'Daylight,' she said. 'Sometimes I get completely confused.'

Ariel nodded confidentially. 'The planet is spinning round and round.'

Cecilia laughed. She didn't really understand why, but at that moment she thought it was especially comical to think that the earth was spinning round and round.

She said, 'Someone or other has said that the world is a stage. In that case it must be a spinning stage.'

'Of course,' decided Ariel. 'But perhaps you don't know why?'

She shrugged her shoulders. 'It doesn't really matter, because I can't feel it spinning. I wouldn't mind if it was even more like a merry-go-round. Supposing it was – it would mean bad times for all the Ferris wheels in the world.'

Ariel got up from the wooden chair, hovered slowly across the room, and sat on the writing desk. He looked down at Cecilia.

'The earth spins so that all the people on earth shall be able to look out into space in all directions. In that way you can take in nearly all the stars and everything out there, no matter where in the world you live.'

'I never thought about that.'

He nodded and went on. 'Whether you live at Jessheim or on Java, not so much as a tiny patch of the glory of heaven will be hidden from you. Besides, it would have been terribly unfair if only half the people on earth were to experience the rays of the sun on their faces; or if, for instance, half of humanity was never able to see so much as a crescent moon. But both the sun and the moon belong to all the people on earth.'

'Was that really why God set the whole whirligig in motion?'

'Yep! But not only because of that . . .'

'Tell me more, then.'

'It was also so that all the angels in heaven should be able to see the whole of the earth, whatever celestial body they happened to find themselves on. You see, it's much easier to keep an eye on a planet that's spinning round and round than on a planet that's turning only one cheek towards you.'

Cecilia thought the angel Ariel was getting almost too enthusiastic. He just talked and talked. Now he had begun swinging his legs too.

'I think I've told you that we have X-ray sight,' he said. 'But I don't think I've said that we have telesight as well.'

'Do you mean that you can see people on earth even when you're sitting on some crazy planet way out in space?'

'Exactly. And up there there isn't so much happening to write home about. But when we're sitting back comfortably on that crazy planet, looking up at the earth, we can watch the heavenly theatre, whether the scenes are taking place in Crete or at Kløfta.'

' "The heavenly theatre"?'

He nodded. 'The world, Cecilia. People's lives on earth are like an endless play. You come and you go. O U T spells out . . .'

Cecilia sat on the edge of her bed for a few seconds without moving. Then she exclaimed, 'That stinks, let me tell you!'

She gave the wooden chair a big kick. 'If it were true, it would be dreadfully unfair.'

Ariel looked slightly taken aback, but it didn't stop him swinging his legs. 'Then we won't talk about it any more,' he said.

'I don't know whether I want to talk any more at all.'

Instantly Ariel stopped swinging his legs. He said, 'You *are* bitter, Cecilia.'

'What if I am?'

'That's why I'm here.'

She stared down at the floor. 'It's just that I can't understand why the world couldn't have been created a *little* differently.'

'We've talked about that already. I'm sure you've tried to draw something well many times, but then it turned out slightly different from what you had in mind.'

'That happens nearly every time. That's what's exciting about it – you don't know exactly what it'll turn into.'

'But then, you haven't complete power over what you draw.'

Cecilia didn't answer. After a long silence she said, 'If I were to draw something, and I knew that what I was drawing would come alive, I wouldn't have dared to draw anything at all. I'd never have dared to give life to something that couldn't defend itself against all those ambitious coloured pencils.'

The angel shrugged his shoulders. 'In any case, the figures you drew would have understood only in part. They would not have seen face to face.'

She gave a deep sigh. 'All these mysteries of yours are beginning to get on my nerves.'

'Pity. Because they're not meant to.'

'Some old codger has said that the most important thing is to be or not to be. I'm more and more in agreement with him. Or with her, of course – but you've said that sex and that sort of thing isn't so important in the spiritual world.'

' "To be or not to be",' repeated Ariel. 'That's well said, for there's nothing in between.'

'I believe we're here on earth only this once. And we shall never return.'

'I know you're very ill, Cecilia – '

She interrupted him. 'But you're not allowed to ask what's the matter with me. Nobody's allowed to talk about it, not even the angels in heaven.'

'I was only going to say that I've come here to comfort you.'

She snorted. 'Comfort!'

Ariel left the writing desk and began hovering round the room while they spoke.

Cecilia said, 'When I'm old and finally die, I believe I'll become a child again. Then I'll go on living in heaven just like you angels. We shall all be like Odin's ravens. And it'll be rather wonderful . . .'

'Do you think so?' asked Ariel.

' "Do you think so? Do you think so?" *You* must know, surely!'

He lay rocking in the air beside the bed, so that he

blocked out the old string of pearls and the Greek calendar with all the cats.

'No way!' he said firmly. 'Both the creation and the heavens are such a great mystery that neither humans on earth nor the angels in heaven can comprehend it.'

'Then I might just as well talk to Father or Grandma.'

He nodded. 'Because they, too, are floating somewhere in God's great mystery.'

She looked up at him. 'Have you met God? In person, I mean.'

'I'm sitting face to face with a tiny part of him now. For whatever I have seen and spoken about with one of his little ones, I have seen it and spoken about it with him.'

Cecilia thought hard. 'If we can only meet God in that way, it would be a bit difficult to get the better of him.'

Ariel couldn't help laughing. 'That would just be him getting the better of himself.'

The room became quite quiet before the angel Ariel continued.

'When you complain that God is stupid, it may be that God is accusing himself. Or have you forgotten what he said as he hung on the cross?'

Cecilia nodded. Grandma had read a great deal to her from the Bible recently, but she had forgotten that bit. 'Tell me, then!'

'He said, "My God, my God, why hast Thou forsaken me?"'

An idea dawned on Cecilia. She had never thought of this. For if Jesus was God, then God had talked to himself as he hung on the cross. Perhaps he was talking to himself when he spoke to the disciples in the Garden of Gethsemane too. They hadn't even bothered to stay awake when he was taken prisoner.

' "My God, my God, why hast Thou forsaken me?" ' she repeated.

Ariel hovered a little closer. He looked into her eyes with his sapphire blue gaze and said, 'Just say it, Cecilia! Just say it over and over again. For there *is* something in the firmament that's not right. Something *has* gone wrong with the whole of the great design.'

She tried to collect her thoughts.

'Don't you really know any more about what's on the other side?' she asked.

He shook his smooth head. 'We see everything in a glass. Now you've glimpsed the other side through the glass. I can't polish the whole looking-glass. If I could, you might have seen even more, but then you would no longer see yourself.'

She stared at him, astonished. 'That was a very deep thought,' she said.

He nodded. 'And you can come no deeper with flesh and blood. For flesh and blood is a shallow pond. I can see the sand and stones at the bottom all the time.'

'Is that true?'

He nodded. 'Flesh and blood are no more than earth

139

and water, after all. But God has breathed some of his spirit into you. That is why there is a part of you that is God.'

Cecilia threw out her arms in desperation.

'I don't know what to say,' she said.

'You could congratulate yourself – '

'It's not my birthday!'

He shook his head. 'You could congratulate yourself because you're a human being who has been part of an extraordinary journey in the firmament round a fiery sun. Here you experienced a fraction of eternity. You have peered out into the universe, Cecilia! That's how you were able to look up from the design of which you are a part. So you were able to see your own great majesty in the enormous looking-glass of heaven.'

Ariel had become so solemn that Cecilia was quite frightened of all his words.

'I don't think you should say a single word more,' she said. 'I don't think I could bear it.'

'Just this!' he said finally. He stared into her eyes with a gaze that was clearer and deeper than the Aegean Sea.

'All stars fall at some time. But a star is only a tiny spark from the great beacon in the sky.'

The next moment he had vanished. At the same time she must have fallen asleep. When she woke again Mother, Father and Grandma were sitting beside her bed.

'Are you all here?'

They nodded, all three. Mother wiped Cecilia's mouth with a damp cloth.

'Where's Lars?'

'Out with Grandad, skating.'

'I want to talk to Grandma.'

'Do you want Father and me to go?'

She nodded. They both tiptoed out. Grandma took her hands.

'Do you remember telling me about Odin?' asked Cecilia.

'Of course I remember.'

'He had two ravens on his shoulders, one on each shoulder. Every single morning they flew out into the world to see how everything was. Then they came home to Odin and told him what they had seen.'

'Now *you*'re telling me the story,' said Grandma.

When Cecilia didn't say anything more, she went on: 'But in a way it was Odin himself who was flying about. Even though he was sitting still on his throne, he was able to flutter about the world on the ravens' wings. And of course, ravens have very good eyesight – '

Cecilia stopped her. 'That was what I wanted to say.'

'What was it?'

'I wish I had two ravens like that. Or at least that I was one of them.'

Grandma squeezed her hands a little tighter. 'We needn't talk about things like that now.'

'Besides, I've started to forget everything you've told me,' said Cecilia.

'I think you remember very well.'

'Did you say that we become sad when something's beautiful? Or did you say that we become beautiful when something's sad?'

Grandma didn't answer. She just held Cecilia's wrists and looked into her eyes.

'There's a notebook under my bed,' said Cecilia. 'Could you pick it up?'

Grandma let go of one of her hands, bent down and picked up the Chinese notebook. She found the black felt pen too.

'Could you write something for me?' asked Cecilia.

Grandma let go of her other hand too, and Cecilia dictated to her:

'We see everything in a glass, darkly. Sometimes we can peer through the glass and catch a glimpse of what is on the other side. If we were to polish the glass clean, we'd see much more. But then we would no longer see ourselves.'

Grandma looked up from the notebook.

'Wasn't that a deep thought?' asked Cecilia.

Grandma nodded, and a few tears ran down her cheeks.

'Are you crying?' asked Cecilia.

'Yes, I'm crying, little one.'

'Because it was so beautiful, or because it was sad?'

'Both.'

'There's more.'

'Just go on talking, then.'

'If I were to draw something, and I knew that what I was drawing would come alive when the drawing was finished, I wouldn't dare to draw anything at all. I would never dare to give life to something that couldn't defend itself against all those ambitious coloured pencils.'

It became quite quiet in the bedroom. It was quite quiet in the rest of the house too.

'What do you think?' asked Cecilia.

'That's fine.'

'Can you write any more?'

Grandma cried again. Then she nodded, and Cecilia dictated:

'Both the creation and the heavens are such a great mystery that neither human beings on earth nor the angels in heaven can comprehend it. But there is something in the firmament that is not quite right. Something has gone wrong with the whole of the great design.'

She looked up. 'Then there's only one thing more.'

Grandma nodded again, and Cecilia said:

'All stars fall at some time. But a star is only a tiny spark from the great beacon in the sky.'

ONE afternoon Cecilia was woken by the blackbird outside. It was Mother who was sitting beside the bed.

'Why is the window open?' she asked.

'It's so lovely and mild outside, almost like spring.'

'Has all the snow gone?'

'Oh no.'

'Is there ice on the river?'

She nodded. 'But it's not so safe any longer.'

Cecilia thought about Ariel. The last time he came he had been so solemn. Could it have been because he had revealed the very last secrets about heavenly things?

There was always somebody sitting with her now. One evening Cecilia asked to be alone during the night. Mother and Father were both sitting with her.

'One of us is here all the time,' Father assured her.

'Why?'

When nobody replied, she said, 'If I want anything I can ring the bell.'

Father stroked her hair. 'You might not manage it.'

'Then I can send an angel to wake you.'

Mother and Father looked at each other.

Cecilia said, 'Surely you don't believe I've thought of running away?'

Father simply shook his head, but Mother said, 'We're sitting with you just as we used to do when you were a baby.'

'Because now you're suddenly afraid that the bird is going to leave the nest?'

She almost had to bully them to leave the room. When she woke a little later, Ariel was sitting on the windowsill.

'You look very beautiful when you're asleep,' he said.

'But I don't want to chat. I want to go out!'

'Can you be bothered?'

'I certainly can! I want to go down and look at the river before the ice melts.'

Ariel sighed. 'It'll be a lot of bother with all those clothes.'

'But I want to go out,' she repeated.

'Just a short while, then.'

He helped her to find her winter clothes in the cupboard.

'And tonight we're taking the toboggan,' she said firmly.

Ariel smiled. 'It'll be the very first time I've gone tobogganing.'

'Or at least, the first time this year,' added Cecilia.

When she had dressed they stood for a while together, examining the beautiful stones on the book-shelf.

'They come from almost all the countries in the world,' she said. 'Every single stone is a tiny fragment of the earth.'

' "A tiny fragment of the earth",' repeated Ariel.

He pointed to the butterfly that Marianne had given Cecilia. 'Not that one, surely?'

She didn't answer, but put it in her anorak pocket. 'It's going out to fly now,' she said.

' "Out to fly",' mimicked Ariel. ' "It's going out to fly now." '

'First you must see if they're all asleep.'

A cunning look came into Ariel's eyes. 'Shall we both have a look?'

They went out into the corridor and put down the toboggan by the stairs. Then they crept into Mother's and Father's bedroom. The door was open. They stood beside each other just inside the door. Cecilia put a finger to her lips.

'Ssh!' she whispered.

The room was almost dark, but a little light was stealing through the window from the lamp above the barn door. Mother and Father were lying close to each other.

'Don't you think they look like little children when they're asleep?' whispered Ariel.

She nodded. 'I wonder what they're dreaming about.'

They went out into the corridor again and into Little Lars's room. A large heap of Lego bricks was lying on the floor. Cecilia had to walk carefully so as not to kick them. Ariel simply rose a few inches above the floor.

She felt so fond of her little brother that she had to dry a few tears from her eyes.

Wasn't it strange that you got tears in your eyes because you were fond of someone? During these past few weeks she had spent so little time with Lars that he had almost become like a stranger to her.

They picked up the toboggan and crept down the stairs to the ground floor.

'Grandma and Grandad live in the little house next door,' whispered Cecilia.

The angel Ariel nodded. 'But Grandma's sleeping on the sofa in the living room at the moment.'

They peeped in, and it was quite true. There was Grandma asleep with all her clothes on and only a little rug over her. Cecilia knew she had slept on the sofa a few times recently. It was because she couldn't stand listening to Grandad snoring, Mother said. *She* said it was because she had to help Mother with the injections.

'She's the grandest grandma in the world,' she whispered.

'I know she is,' replied Ariel.

'Not just because she's my grandma. She *is* the grandest grandma in the world.'

' "Grandest grandma",' mimicked Ariel. ' "The grandest grandma in the world".'

They went out on to the steps and closed the outer door behind them. Outside it was a cold winter's night. The sky was so full of sparkling stars that it was as light as an eighth of daylight. There was no moon, so the stars were unusually clear. Only when it was completely dark did the darkness show all their rays.

Cecilia ran across the yard pulling the toboggan behind her. Grandma had tied a thick rope to it. Mother had said there was no hurry. So Cecilia and Grandma had done it secretly.

Long, gentle slopes stretched from the yard almost all the way to the river. Cecilia sat on the toboggan at once. As she set off she turned to Ariel and called, 'If you want to come with me, hold tight!'

He followed and sat close behind her. The surface was icy, so they went down the meadow at a terrific speed. The toboggan didn't stop until they were right at the bottom beside the thicket on the river bank.

Cecilia laughed. 'A record!' she said.

She stood up and turned to Ariel. 'Wasn't that marvellous?'

'I'm sure it was,' he replied, with a sad expression, 'but I didn't feel anything.'

'Now we'll cross the river,' decided Cecilia. She began pushing her way through the thicket. Then they were out on the ice.

'I wasn't given skates,' she said, 'but I can go skating all the same!'

She let go of the toboggan and started to slide on her

boots across the ice. Ariel followed her on his bare feet. They must have been very smooth, because he made a few funny pirouettes on the ice just like an ice-dancer.

All of a sudden a growling and screeching came from the ice. Cecilia ran over to the other bank as fast as she could. Ariel came fluttering after her. When they turned and looked back, they discovered that the ice had broken into several big floes. Out in the middle of the river lay the toboggan on one of them.

'The toboggan!' she called.

She didn't need to say any more, for Ariel was already on his way. Cecilia thought he was going to hover above the river and then dive down and grab it. But when he reached the river bank he simply went on walking on the ice floes. In some places he walked on the water as well.

He was back with the toboggan in no time. Cecilia couldn't quite make out what was happening, but it almost looked as if it was hovering above the water the way the Christmas *nisse*'s reindeer pull a sled through the air.

'Super!' she exclaimed.

She seized the toboggan rope firmly and said, 'We're going to visit Marianne!'

They jogged up the slope to the yellow house. Cecilia hadn't been there for months. Marianne had come to visit her several times before Christmas, but many weeks had passed since then.

As soon as they reached the house, Cecilia tried the door. It was locked.

'Then we can't get in,' decided Ariel. 'Of course I could get through the door, but I don't think both of us should do it.'

Cecilia smiled cunningly. She began walking towards the outhouse and beckoned to Ariel to follow.

'I know where they keep the key,' she said proudly.

She found it immediately, under an empty paint can. At times she had visited Marianne as often as she had been at home at Skotbu.

She unlocked the door of the house and they crept inside. To get to Marianne's room they had to go through the living room. Cecilia switched on a wall lamp. Ariel followed her like a younger brother.

She turned the handle cautiously and opened the door. Marianne was lying asleep with her long red hair spread out on the pillow. Cecilia had felt as free and happy as a bird all this time, but when she saw Marianne she shed a tear. Perhaps it was because she was asleep, or because it had been so long since she had seen her.

'Are you crying?' whispered Ariel.

'Yes, I'm crying.'

Marianne began turning over in bed. It looked as if she might wake up at any moment. Ariel tugged at Cecilia's anorak. 'You must say goodbye to her now!'

Cecilia opened her anorak pocket and took out the little butterfly. She leaned over cautiously and placed it carefully on the floor beside Marianne's bed.

'Why did you do that?' asked Ariel. '*She* gave it to you.'

She sighed. 'Oh, I don't suppose I'll have any use for it after all.'

The next moment her friend sat up in bed, but by then Cecilia and Ariel were on their way out through the living room. They locked the outer door behind them, and Cecilia ran into the outhouse with the key. Then they sat on the toboggan and slid the short distance back to the river.

When the toboggan had come to a stop, Ariel jumped up and began hovering around her like a weightless doll. Cecilia felt a little weightless herself. She sat on the toboggan, staring up at the starry sky.

'This is eternity,' she sighed.

'Or heaven,' said the angel Ariel. 'Or the firmament.'

'Or the universe,' continued Cecilia.

'Or the cosmos,' said Ariel, and they were both on the brink of laughter.

'Or space!'

'Or the salt of the earth!'

'Or reality!'

'Or simply the world!'

'Or The Great Mystery!' exclaimed Cecilia finally.

Ariel nodded solemnly. 'An orphan child has many names.'

'An orphan child?'

He nodded again. 'It's not the loved children who are

given many names. It's the lost children. The ones who are found on the doorsteps. The ones who come from nobody knows where. The ones who hover in empty space.'

'This is eternity,' repeated Cecilia.

The angel Ariel fluttered down on to the toboggan beside her. Then he said, 'And you see that most clearly in the middle of the night.'

Cecilia turned towards him and repeated something that she had said once before. This time she said it stressing every single syllable.

'I am here only this once. And I shall never return.'

But the angel Ariel shook his head.

He said, 'You are in eternity now. And that returns for ever and ever.'

They walked down to the river bank and saw how the large ice floes were being slowly pushed along through the valley. The river, which had been lying so still and peaceful all the winter, was suddenly making angry sounds. They followed the river down to the bridge and began to cross over to the other side.

When they got to the middle of the bridge, Ariel pointed down at the water and asked, 'What exactly is this river called?'

' "What exactly is this river called?" ' she repeated. 'I've told you lots of times already. It's called Leira.'

He nodded. 'That's a beautiful name. And very earthly, because it makes me think of clay. But in a heavenly looking-glass even the most earthly thing becomes heavenly as well.'

'I don't understand you.'

'Leira . . .' repeated Ariel.

He smiled mysteriously. 'You see everything in a glass, darkly.'

She shrugged her shoulders. Then Ariel said, 'Can you read "Leira" backwards?'

There was a second's pause.

'ARIEL!' exclaimed Cecilia. 'Of course! It's Ariel!'

He nodded proudly. 'I've always liked it in this valley.'

Cecilia was mightily impressed.

As they walked uphill towards Skotbu she tilted her head back several times and gazed up at the universe. Suddenly they caught sight of a shooting star. Ariel put his hand to his mouth and said, 'A star is falling.'

' "A star is falling," ' repeated Cecilia.

She was reminded of the old Christmas tree star that had suddenly disappeared. Hadn't Ariel said once that he knew where it was?

As she pulled the toboggan after her and tramped up the last stretch towards the red barn at Skotbu, she turned to him and asked, 'Do you remember I told you about the old Christmas tree star which disappeared in such a mysterious way?'

He had a strange look on his face. 'It may not be so mysterious after all.'

'Exactly!' replied Cecilia. 'Because *you* know where it is.'

She felt cold. What had Ariel meant when he said it wasn't so mysterious after all? And if he had known where it was all the time, why hadn't he told her long before now?

They had reached the yard.

'Come here,' said the angel Ariel, and pointed behind the barn.

A few branches of a withered tree were sticking out right beside the barn wall. Nearly all the needles had fallen off. Those that were left were all a light brown colour. Clearly the tree had been lying under the snow all winter. Now the thaw had begun, and the withered tree had appeared again.

'It's last year's Christmas tree!' exclaimed Cecilia.

She remembered that she had put it there with Father just over a year ago.

Ariel kicked aside a little loose snow and pulled the tree free. Then Cecilia caught sight of the old star. It was still tied to the top of the tree. Imagine not having thought of that! Imagine nobody thinking that they might simply have forgotten the star when they took down the decorations!

The withered bush looked sad and pathetic. It made Cecilia think of the black lava beach on the island of Santorini. Only the star was still the same. The winter had done it no harm. It was still undamaged.

The angel Ariel bent down and touched the star with

154

his finger. It began to shine as if it had an electric current in it.

Cecilia was enchanted. 'How beautiful!'

As soon as Ariel took his finger away from the star, it faded.

'Do it again!' she begged.

So he did. It was enough for him barely to touch the old Christmas tree star for it to light up again and shine on Cecilia and Ariel, the barn wall and the snowdrifts around them.

Ariel gestured to her. She understood that they must go indoors and up to her bedroom before anyone in the house woke up.

He helped her into bed this time too. He leant the toboggan against the wall exactly where it had been before. Then he blew the room quite clean of snow and slush. Cecilia slept the instant she lay down.

When she woke, Father and Grandma were sitting beside her.

'Night?' she asked.

Father nodded. He took her hands while Grandma wiped her lips.

'I know what happened to the old Christmas tree star,' she whispered.

Grandma and Father looked at each other.

'The Christmas tree star?' repeated Father.

She nodded. 'It's lying behind the barn. We forgot to take it down with the other decorations.'

Before Cecilia slept again she looked up at Grandma,

and said a few words as loudly and clearly as she could. She spoke them as if they were taken from a poem she had once learned by heart.

'It's not the loved children who are given many names. It's the lost children. Those who are found on doorsteps. Those who come from nobody knows where. Those who hover in empty space.'

C ECILIA woke up suddenly and opened her eyes wide. She turned towards Father who was sitting on the chair beside the bed. He had the old Christmas tree star in his hand.

She didn't quite know why, but it made her so incredibly glad that they had believed her. They had actually gone behind the barn, where she had been in the night with the angel Ariel, and found the star.

'You found it where I said it was,' she mumbled. It was a bit difficult to get the words out.

Father put it on her duvet.

'How did you know it was still on the Christmas tree?' he whispered.

She tried to smile. 'One of God's angels told me.'

'We found it exactly where you said it was.'

'But you can't make it shine. Only God can do that.'

Now Mother and Grandma had come into the room. And then Grandad came too. They must have been standing in the passage outside, and had come in when they heard her talking about the angel who had helped her.

She looked up at them. She felt much clearer in her head today than she had for some time. If only she weren't so weak . . .

There were two chairs beside the bed. Mother sat down on the extra one, Grandma and Grandad stood behind her, looking down at Cecilia. Of the four of them, only Grandma was smiling.

'Would you like to say hello to Little Lars?' asked Mother.

Cecilia nodded. Grandma went out to fetch him. She had to push him in front of her because he was so shy.

'Hi,' he said.

'Hi, Little Lars.'

She looked up. 'How are the mini-skis going?'

'Fine.'

When nobody said anything more, she tried to say something funny.

'By the way, you should tidy up your room, lazy-bones.'

They all smiled, even though it wasn't so very funny after all. Only Cecilia could know that she had been in his room during the night.

She said, 'The ice is leaving the river.'

They nodded, and it was quiet for a long time.

It felt as if her last words were singing in her ears long after she had spoken them: 'The ice is leaving the river.' 'The ice is leaving . . .'

'Imagine finding the old Christmas tree star again,' said Grandma. 'We've all been behind the barn.'

'We've all been behind the barn.'

Imagine them doing that! All of them. They had stood poking about in the snow just like Cecilia and Ariel.

'But you won't find the fever butterfly,' she said proudly. 'Because it's flown away.'

Mother got up from her chair and began to cross the room. Was she going to try to find the butterfly on the bookshelf?

But Grandma stopped her before she got that far. 'Antonia!' she said, and gestured to her to sit down.

Another long pause followed before anyone said anything.

Cecilia thought it was strange that her head could be so clear and yet she should only want to sleep.

'I think I'll go to sleep again,' she whispered. 'So I'll just say 'bye for now.'

When she woke a little later the window was open and nobody was sitting beside the bed.

Soon the angel Ariel floated in through the open window, and sat on the writing desk. Cecilia got out of bed and stood upright.

'Are you back again?' she asked.

He didn't reply directly. 'Would you like to come out with me and fly?'

She laughed. 'But *I* can't fly.'

The angel Ariel sighed indulgently. 'It's time to finish with all that nonsense. Just come here.'

So Cecilia went towards the angel Ariel.

He took her hand. The next moment they were in free flight through the open window, over the barn, and above the whole landscape. It was early in the morning just before sunrise on a new winter's day.

'Marvellous!' said Cecilia. 'Quite angelically marvellous!'

It was even more wonderful to fly than she had imagined. She felt a tickling in her stomach when she looked down at the pointed tips of the fir trees. When she lifted her head she could see for miles in every direction. She pointed down at the airport and Witches' Hill, at Lake Hurdal and Lake Mjøsa. She could even see the Oslofjord far away, and glimpse the sea in the distance.

They circled high above Ravens' Hill. From here it looked like a little pile of sugar.

She said, 'Now we're just like Odin's ravens.'

'Exactly,' replied the angel Ariel. 'And when we sit at God's right hand, we shall tell him about everything we've seen.'

A little later they flew back to the open window and sat on the windowsill, just as Ariel had done the first time he came.

They both looked down at her bed. Cecilia didn't think it at all strange that she could see herself lying there with her fair hair over the pillow. On the duvet they had placed the old Christmas tree star.

'I agree that I look beautiful when I'm asleep,' she said.

Ariel was holding her hand tightly. He looked up at her and said, 'You're even more beautiful sitting here.'

'But I can't see that for myself, because now I'm on the other side of the looking-glass.'

As soon as she said that, Ariel let go of her hand.

He said, 'You look like a splendid butterfly that has flown from the hand of God.'

She looked at the room. A narrow strip of morning sun had fallen on the writing desk and the floor. Under Cecilia's bed a few rays had found their way to the Chinese notebook. She saw how all the silken threads shone and glittered.

ALSO AVAILABLE IN PHOENIX PAPERBACK
The International Bestseller

Sophie's World

Looking in her mailbox one day, fourteen-year-old Sophie Amundsen finds two surprising pieces of paper. On them are written the questions: 'Who are you?' and 'Where does the world come from?'. The writer is an enigmatic philosopher called Albert Knox and his two teasing questions are the beginning of a tour through the history of Western Philosophy from the pre-Socratics to Sartre. In a series of brilliantly entertaining letters, and then in person, Albert Knox opens Sophie's enquiring mind to the fundamental questions that philosophers have been asking since the dawn of civilisation. But as soon as Sophie begins to find her feet in this dazzling, exciting new world, she and Albert find themselves caught up in a plot which is itself a most perplexing philosophical conundrum . . .

PRICE: £6.99

ISBN: 1 85799 291 1

ALSO AVAILABLE IN PHOENIX PAPERBACK

The Solitaire Mystery

Twelve-year-old Hans Thomas and his father are on a journey to Greece in search of the boy's mother when a series of unusual incidents occurs: a dwarf gives Hans Thomas a magnifying glass; a baker gives him a bun containing a miniature book that tells the story of a sailor shipwrecked on a desert island; a pack of playing cards seems to have a life of its own; and what of the Joker who looks too deeply and too much?

PRICE: £6.99

ISBN: 1 85799 865 0

ALSO AVAILABLE IN PHOENIX PAPERBACK

Vita Brevis

In a second-hand bookshop in Buenos Aires, Jostein Gaarder makes an exciting find: a transcript of a letter to St Augustine, author of the famous *Confessions*, from Floria Aemilia, the woman he renounced for chastity. *Vita Brevis* is both a classic love story, beautifully told, and a fascinating insight into St Augustine's life and that of his discarded concubine. It is up to the reader to determine its authenticity . . .

PRICE: £5.99
ISBN:0 75380 461 1

All Orion/Phoenix titles are available at your local bookshop or from the following address:

Littlehampton Book Services
Cash Sales Department L
14 Eldon Way, Lineside Industrial Estate
Littlehampton
West Sussex BN17 7HE

telephone 01903 721596, *facsimile* 01903 730914

Payment can either be made by credit card (Visa and Mastercard accepted) or by sending a cheque or postal order made payable to *Littlehampton Book Services*.
DO NOT SEND CASH OR CURRENCY.

Please add the following to cover postage and packing

UK and BFPO:
£1.50 for the first book, and 50p for each additional book to a maximum of £3.50

Overseas and Eire:
£2.50 for the first book plus £1.00 for the second book and 50p for each additional book ordered

----

BLOCK CAPITALS PLEASE

name of cardholder ....   *delivery address*
                     ....   *(if different from cardholder)*
address of cardholder ....
....
....
....
        postcode ....   *postcode* ....

☐ I enclose my remittance for £...............................

☐ please debit my Mastercard/Visa (delete as appropriate)

card number ☐☐☐☐☐☐☐☐☐☐☐☐☐☐☐☐☐

expiry date ☐☐☐☐

signature ....

prices and availability are subject to change without notice